THE WIND LIFTED INTO HIS FACE, BLOWING ASIDE HIS HEADCLOTH AND THE SUN CUT SHARPLY AGAINST THE UNPROTECTED FLESH, AND THEN HE WAS ON HIS FACE IN THE SAND AND JAMAL WAS LIFTING HIM AGAIN.

Later, he was lying across the Somali's broad shoulders, and he frowned and shook his head trying to think clearly, but it was no good. Nothing was any good now, and he lapsed into a dark vacuum of heat.

There was sand in his mouth and his fingers clawed at the ground but this time no hand lifted him in its strong grip. This time he was on his own. Utterly and finally alone ...

Jack Higgins was raised in Belfast in a family with a political background and frequently experienced the worst aspect of the troubles during his youth. He later moved to Leeds, left school with no qualifications and had a succession of jobs, including two years as an NCO in the Royal Horse Guards serving on the East German border during the Cold War. He was then accepted as an external student at London University while working as a circus tent-hand, a tram conductor and most things in between, and a degree in sociology and social psychology took him into teaching before he became a full-time author. He was already a writer of adventure stories when he wrote *The Eagle Has Landed* but his highly original war novel turned him into an international bestselling author. His novels have since sold over 250 million copies and have been translated into forty-four languages. Many of them have been filmed. The most notable being *The Eagle Has Landed*, *Confessional*, *Night of the Fox*, which was made into a highly successful ITV series, *A Season in Hell*, *Cold Harbour*, *The Eagle Has Flown* and *On Dangerous Ground*.

Other Jack Higgins books published by Signet are *Eye of the Storm*, *Thunderpoint* and *On Dangerous Ground*.

JACK HIGGINS

SHEBA

A SIGNET BOOK

SIGNET

Published by the Penguin Group
Penguin Books Ltd, 27 Wrights Lane, London W8 5TZ, England
Penguin Books USA Inc., 375 Hudson Street, New York, New York 10014, USA
Penguin Books Australia Ltd, Ringwood, Victoria, Australia
Penguin Books Canada Ltd, 10 Alcorn Avenue, Toronto, Ontario, Canada M4V 3B2
Penguin Books (NZ) Ltd, 182–190 Wairau Road, Auckland 10, New Zealand

Penguin Books Ltd, Registered Offices: Harmondsworth, Middlesex, England

First published in Great Britain by Michael Joseph, 1994
Published in Signet 1995
7 9 10 8 6

Copyright © Jack Higgins, 1994
All rights reserved

In 24 BC *the Roman General, Aelius Gallus, tried to conquer Southern Arabia and succeeded only in losing most of his army in the awesome region known as the Empty Quarter, the Rubh al Khali. Amongst the survivors was a Greek adventurer named Alexias, centurion in the Tenth Legion, who walked out of the desert carrying with him a secret of the ancient world as astonishing as King Solomon's Mines, a secret that was lost for two thousand years. Until . . .*

BERLIN

....

March 1939

ONE

AS RAIN DRIFTED across Berlin in a great curtain on the final evening of March a black Mercedes limousine moved along Wilhelmstrasse towards the new Reich Chancellery which had only opened in January. Hitler had given them a year to complete the project. His orders had been obeyed with two weeks to spare. Admiral Wilhelm Canaris, Chief of Military Intelligence, the Abwehr, leaned forward and wound down the window so that he could obtain a better view.

He shook his head. 'Incredible. Do you realize, Hans, that the frontage on Voss–Strasse alone is a quarter of a mile long.'

The young man who sat next to him was his aide, a Luftwaffe captain named Hans Ritter. He had an Iron Cross Second and First Class and was handsome enough until he turned his head and the dreadful burn scar was visible on his right cheek; and there was a walking stick on the floor at his feet, the unfortunate result of his having been shot down by an American volunteer pilot while flying with the German Condor Legion in the Spanish Civil War.

'With all those pillars, Herr Admiral, the marble, it's more like some marvel of the ancient world.'

'Instead of a symbol of the new order?' Canaris shrugged and wound up the window. 'Everything passes, Hans, even the Third Reich although our beloved Führer has given us a thousand years.' He took a cigarette from his case and Ritter gave him a light, as always slightly alarmed at the mocking in the older man's voice.

'As you say, Herr Admiral.'

'Yes, it's a bizarre thought, isn't it? One day people could be wandering around what's left of the Chancellery, tourists, just like they inspect the ruins of the Temple of Luxor in Egypt saying: "I wonder what they were like?"'

Ritter was thoroughly uncomfortable now as the Mercedes drove through the gilded gates into a court of honour and moved towards the steps leading up to the massive entrance. 'If the Herr Admiral could give me an idea of why we've been called.'

'I haven't the slightest notion and it's me he wants to see, not you, Hans. I simply want you on hand if anything unusual turns up.'

'Shall I wait in the car?' Ritter asked as they pulled up at the bottom of the steps.

'No, you can wait in reception. Much more comfortable and you'll be able to feast on the new art forms of the Third Reich. Vulgar, but sustaining.'

The Kriegsmarine Petty Officer who was his driver ran round to open the door. Canaris got out and waited courteously for Ritter, who had considerably more difficulty. His left leg was false from the knee down, but once on his feet he moved quite well with the aid of his stick and they went up the steps together.

The SS guards were troops of the Leibstandarte Adolf Hitler and wore black dress uniform and full white leather harness. They saluted smartly as Canaris and Ritter passed inside. The hall was truly remarkable with mosaic floor, doors seventeen feet high and great eagles carrying swastikas in their claws. A young Hauptsturm-führer in dress uniform sat at a gold desk, two orderlies standing behind. He jumped to his feet.

'Herr Admiral. The Führer has asked for you twice.'

'My dear Hoffer, I didn't get his summons until half an hour ago,' Canaris said. 'Not that that will do me any good. This is my aide, Captain Ritter. Look after him for me.'

'Of course, Herr Admiral.' Hoffer nodded to one of the orderlies. 'Take the Herr Admiral to the Führer's reception suite.'

The orderly set off at a sharp pace and Canaris went

after him. Hoffer came round the desk and said to Ritter, 'Spain?'

'Yes.' Ritter tapped his false foot. 'I could still fly, but they won't let me.'

'What a pity,' Hoffer said and led him over to the seating area. 'You'll miss the big show.'

'You think it will come?' Ritter asked, easing himself down and taking out his cigarette case.

'Don't you? And by the way, no smoking. Führer's express order.'

'Damn!' Ritter said, for his pain was constant and cigarettes helped.

'Sorry,' Hoffer said sympathetically. 'But coffee we do have and it's the best.'

He turned, went to his desk and picked up the phone.

When the guard opened the enormous door to Hitler's study, Canaris was surprised at the number of people in the room. There were the three commanders-in-chief, Goering for the Luftwaffe, Brauchitsch for the Army and Raeder for the Kriegsmarine. There was Himmler, von Ribbentrop, generals like Jodl, Keitel and Halder. There was a heavy silence and heads turned as Canaris entered.

'Now that the Admiral has deigned to join us we can begin,' Hitler said; 'and I will be brief. As you know the British today gave the Poles an unconditional guarantee of their full support in the event of war.'

Goering said. 'Will the French follow, my Führer?'

'Undoubtedly,' Hitler told him. 'But they will do nothing when it comes to the crunch.'

'You mean, invade Poland?' Halder, who was Chief of Staff at OKW, said. 'What about the Russians?'

'They won't interfere. Let us say there are negotiations in hand and leave it at that. So, gentlemen, my will is fixed in this matter. You will prepare Case White, the invasion of Poland on September the 1st.'

There were shocked gasps. 'But my Führer, that only gives us six months,' Colonel-General von Brauchitsch protested.

'Ample time,' Hitler told him. 'If there are those who disagree, speak now.' There was a profound silence. 'Good, then get to work, gentlemen. You may all leave except for you, Herr Admiral.'

They all filed out and Canaris stood there waiting while Hitler looked out of the window at the rain. Finally he turned. 'The British and the French will declare war, but they won't do anything. Do you agree?'

'Absolutely,' Canaris said.

'We smash Poland, wrap things up in a few weeks. Once it's done, what is the point of the British and French continuing? They'll sue for peace.'

'And if not?'

Hitler shrugged. 'Then I'll have Case Yellow implemented. We'll invade Belgium, Holland, France and drive the English into the sea. They'll come to their senses then. After all, they are not our natural enemies.'

'I agree,' Canaris said.

'Having said that, it occurs to me that I should demonstrate to our English friends as soon as possible that I *do* mean business.'

Canaris cleared his throat. 'Exactly what do you have in mind, my Führer?'

Hitler gestured towards the huge map of the world that hung on the far wall. 'Come over here, Herr Admiral, and let me show you.'

When Canaris returned to the reception hall at the Chancellery an hour later, Hoffer was seated behind his desk with the two orderlies. There was no sign of Ritter. The SS Captain stood up and came to greet him.

'Herr Admiral.'

'My aide?' Canaris asked.

'Hauptman Ritter was badly in need of a smoke. He went back to your car.'

'My thanks,' Canaris said. 'I'll find my own way.'

He went out of the huge doors and stood at the top of the steps, buttoning his greatcoat, looking out at the rain. He went down the steps and had the rear door of the limousine open before his driver realized what was happening, and climbed in beside Ritter.

8

'My office,' he called to the driver, then closed the glass partition.

Ritter started to stub out his cigarette as they drove away, and Canaris sat back. 'Never mind. Just give me one of those things. I need it.'

Ritter got his cigarette case out and offered a light. 'Is everything all right, Herr Admiral? I saw them all leave. I was worried.'

'The Führer, Hans, gave us his personal order to invade Poland on September the 1st.'

'My God,' Ritter said. 'Case White.'

'Exactly. He has been negotiating with the Russians, who will do a deal. They'll let us get on with it in return for a slice of eastern Poland.'

'And the British?'

'Oh, they'll declare war and I'm sure the French will go along. The Führer, however, is convinced they will do nothing on the Western Front and for once I agree. They'll sit there while we wrap up Poland, and his feeling is that once it's an accomplished fact, we can all get round the negotiating table and get back to the status quo. Britain, as he informed us, is not our natural enemy.'

'Do you agree, Herr Admiral?'

'He's right enough there, but the British are a stubborn lot, Hans, and Chamberlain is not popular. Since Munich his own people despise him.' Canaris stubbed out his cigarette. 'If there was a change at the top, Churchill for example . . .' He shrugged. 'Who knows?'

'And what would we do?'

'Implement Case Yellow. Invade the Low Countries and France and drive whatever army the British had brought across the channel into the sea.'

There was a pause before Ritter said, 'Could this be done?'

'I think so, Hans, as long as the Americans don't interfere. Under the Führer's inspired leadership we have reoccupied the Rhineland, absorbed Austria and Czecho-slovakia plus one or two bits and pieces. I have no doubt we'll win in Poland.'

'But afterwards, Herr Admiral? The French, the British?'

'Ah, well now we come down to why the Führer kept me back when everyone else left.'

'A special project, Herr Admiral?'

'You could say that. He wants us to blow up the Suez Canal on the 1st of September, the day we invade Poland.'

Ritter, in the act of snapping his cigarette case open, said, 'Good God!'

Canaris took the case from him and helped himself. 'He got the idea from this Colonel Rommel who com-manded the Führer's escort battalion for the occupation of the Sudetenland. He thinks highly of Colonel

Rommel and with reason and there is a certain mad logic to the idea. I mean, the Suez Canal is the direct link to the British Empire. Cut it and all shipping to India, the Far East and Australia would have to go by way of Africa and the Cape of Good Hope. The military implications speak for themselves.'

'But Herr Admiral, how on earth would we get men and equipment into the area?'

Canaris shook his head. 'No, Hans, you've got it wrong. We're not talking direct military action here, we're talking sabotage. The Führer wants us, the Abwehr, to blow up the Suez Canal on the day we invade Poland. Put the damn thing out of action. Close it down so fully that it would take a year or so to open it again.'

'What a coup. It would shock the world,' Ritter said.

'More to the point, it would shock the British to the core and make them realize we mean business. At least that's the way our beloved Führer sees it.' Canaris sighed. 'Of course, how the hell we are to accomplish this is another matter, but we'll have to come up with something, at least on paper, and that's where you come in, Hans.'

'I see, Herr Admiral.'

The limousine pulled in to the kerb outside the Abwehr offices at 74-6 Tirpitz Ufer. The Petty Officer hurried round to open the door for Canaris and Ritter scrambled out after him. The young Luftwaffe officer was frowning slightly.

Canaris said, 'Are you all right?'

'Fine, Herr Admiral. It's just that there's something stirring at the back of my mind, something that could suit our purposes.'

'Really?' Canaris smiled and led the way up the steps, pausing at the door. 'Well, that is good news, but sooner rather than later, Hans, remember that,' and he led the way inside.

It was perhaps an hour later and Canaris was seated at his desk working his way through a mass of papers, his two favourite dachshunds asleep in their basket in the corner, when there was a knock at the door and Ritter entered with a file in one hand and a rolled-up map under his arm. He limped forward, leaning on his stick.

'Could I have a word, Herr Admiral, on this Suez Canal venture?'

Canaris sat back. 'So soon, Hans?'

'As I said, there was something at the back of my mind, and when I got to my office I remembered. A report I received last month from a professor of archaeology here at the University, Professor Otto Muller. He's recently returned from Southern Arabia. Intends to go back there soon. He needs additional funding.'

'And what has this to do with us?' Canaris asked.

'As the Herr Admiral knows, all German citizens working abroad have to make a report to us here at Abwehr Headquarters of anything of an unusual nature that they may have come across.'

'So?'

'Allow me, Herr Admiral.' Ritter went across to the map board on the far wall, unrolled the map under his arm and pinned it in place. It showed Egypt and the Suez Canal, the whole of Southern Arabia, the Red Sea and the Gulf of Aden. 'As you can see, Herr Admiral, the British in Aden, the Yemen and then various Arab states along the Gulf of Aden and the Indian Ocean, Dhofar and the Oman.'

'Well?' Canaris asked, examining the map.

'You will notice Dahrein, a port on the Gulf coast. This is where Muller was working from. It belongs to Spain. Rather like Goa on the Indian coast. The Spaniards have been there for four hundred years.'

'I can imagine what the place is like,' Canaris said.

'North across the border with Saudi Arabia is the Rubh al Khali, the Empty Quarter, one of the most awesome deserts on earth.'

'And this is where Muller was operating?'

'Yes, Herr Admiral.'

'But what on earth was he doing?'

'There are remains of many ancient civilizations in the area, inscriptions and graffiti on the rocks. Muller is an expert on ancient languages. He uses a latex solution to take impressions, which are brought back here to the University.'

'And what has this to do with the Suez Canal, Hans?'

'Bear with me, Herr Admiral. The area around there called Saba has long been associated with the Queen of Sheba.'

'My God,' Canaris said and returned to his desk. 'Now it's the Bible.' He took a cigarette from a silver box. 'I always understood that except for the biblical reference there has never been actual proof that she existed.'

'Oh, she did exist, I can assure you,' Ritter said. 'There was a cult of the Arabian goddess, Asthar, their equivalent of Venus. In legend, the Queen of Sheba was high priestess of that cult and built a temple out there in the Empty Quarter.'

'In legend,' Canaris said.

'Muller has found what he thinks could be the ruins of it, Herr Admiral. Naturally he kept his discovery quiet. Such an event would rival the discovery of Tutankhamen's tomb in the Valley of the Kings. Archaeologists would descend from all over the world. As I said, he returned to Berlin for funding, but made a full description of his find in his report to Abwehr.'

Canaris frowned. 'But where is this leading?'

'This place is unknown, Herr Admiral, hidden out

there in the desert. Used for supplies, an aircraft, it could provide a base for a strike against the Canal.'

Canaris got up and went to the map. He examined it and turned. 'A thousand miles at least from that area to the Suez Canal.'

'More like twelve hundred, Herr Admiral, but I'm sure I could find a way.'

Canaris smiled. 'You usually can, Hans. All right, bring Muller to see me.'

'When, Herr Admiral?'

'Why now, of course, tonight. I intend to sleep in the office anyway.'

He returned to his papers and Ritter went out.

Professor Otto Muller was a small, balding man with a wizened face tanned to the shade of old leather by constant exposure to the desert sun. When Ritter ushered him into the office to meet Canaris, Muller smiled nervously, exposing gold-capped teeth.

Canaris said, 'That will do, Hans.' Ritter went out and Canaris lit a cigarette. 'So, Professor, a remarkable find. Tell me about it.'

Muller stood there like a nervous schoolboy. 'I was lucky, Herr Admiral. I've been working in the Shabwa area for some time and one night an old Bedouin staggered into my camp dying of thirst and fever. I nursed him back to life.'

'I see.'

'They're a strange people. Can't bear to be in debt so he repaid me by telling me where Sheba's temple was.'

'Payment indeed. Tell me about it.'

'I first saw it as an outcrop of reddish stone, out there in the vastness of the Empty Quarter. The Herr Admiral must understand that there are sand dunes out there that are hundreds of feet high.'

'Remarkable.'

'As I got closer we entered a gorge. I had two Bedouin with me as guards. We had journeyed by camel. There was a flat plain, very hard-baked, then a gorge, a broad avenue of pillars.'

'And the temple? Tell me about that.'

Which Muller did, talking for a good half-hour while Canaris listened intently. Finally the Admiral nodded. 'Fascinating. Captain Ritter tells me you made an excellent report to Abwehr.'

'I hope I know my duty, Herr Admiral, I'm a party member.'

'Indeed,' Canaris observed drily. 'Then you will no doubt be pleased to return to this place with suitable funding and do what you are told to do. This is a project the Führer himself is interested in.'

Muller drew himself up. 'At your orders, Herr Admiral.'

'Good.' Canaris pressed a button on his desk. 'We'll keep you informed.'

Ritter entered. 'Herr Admiral?'

'Wait outside, Professor,' Canaris said, and waited until Muller had gone out. 'He seems harmless enough, but I still have my doubts, Hans. If you used this place as a base it would require a flight of say twelve hundred miles to the Canal and what real damage could one bomber do? In fact, do we have a plane that could make the flight?'

'I've already had a thought,' Ritter said, 'but I'd like to explore it further before sharing it with you.'

Canaris frowned. 'Is this serious business, Hans?'

'I believe it could be, Herr Admiral.'

'So be it.' Canaris nodded. 'I don't need to tell you to squeeze Muller dry, details of this Dahrein place, how the Spanish run it and so on. At least they're on our side, which could be useful.'

'I'll see to it, sir.'

'At your soonest, Hans. A feasibility study. I'll give you three days.'

Ritter turned and limped out and Canaris went back to his papers.

TWO

ON WEDNESDAY MORNING Canaris, after sleeping once again on the little military bed in his office, was in the bathroom shaving when there was a knock at the door.

'Come in,' he called.

'It's me, Herr Admiral,' Ritter replied. 'And your breakfast.'

Canaris wiped his face and went out to the aroma of good coffee, and found an orderly arranging a tray on his desk, Ritter standing by the window.

'Dismissed,' Canaris said, and picked up his cup as the orderly went out. 'Join me, Hans.'

'I've already had breakfast, Herr Admiral.'

'You must have risen early. How conscientious of you.'

'Not really, Herr Admiral. It's just that I find difficulty sleeping.'

Canaris was immediately all sympathy. 'My dear

Hans, how stupid of me. I'm afraid I often forget just how difficult life must be for you.'

'The fortunes of war, Herr Admiral.' He laid a file on the desk as Canaris buttered some toast. The Admiral looked up. 'What's this?'

'Operation Sheba, Herr Admiral.'

'You mean you've come up with a solution?'

'I believe so.'

'You think this thing could be done?'

'Not only could it be done, Herr Admiral, I think it should be done.'

'Really.' Canaris poured coffee into the spare cup. 'Then I insist that you have a cigarette and drink that while I see what you've got here.'

Ritter did as he was told and limped across to the window. The 3rd of April. Soon it would be Easter and yet it rained like a bad day in November. His leg hurt, but he was damned if he was going to take a morphine pill unless he really had to. He swallowed the coffee and lit a cigarette. Behind him he heard Canaris lift the telephone.

'The Reich Chancellery, the Führer's suite,' the Admiral said, and added after a moment, 'Good morning. Canaris. I must see the Führer. Yes, most urgent.' There was a longer pause and then he said, 'Excellent. Eleven o'clock.'

Ritter turned. 'Herr Admiral?'

'Excellent, Hans, this plan of yours. You can come with me and tell the man yourself.'

Ritter had never ventured beyond the main reception area at the Chancellery before and what he saw was breathtaking, not only the huge doors and bronze eagles but the Marble Gallery, which was four hundred and eighty feet long, the Führer's special pride as it was twice as long as the Hall of Mirrors at Versailles.

When they were admitted to the Führer's enormous study they found Hitler seated at his desk. He looked up. 'Something important, I trust.'

'I think so, my Führer,' Canaris said. 'This is my aide, Captain Ritter.'

Hitler took in the scarred face, the stick, the medals, rose, came round the table and took Ritter's hand. 'As a soldier I salute you.'

He went back to his chair and Ritter, overwhelmed, stammered, 'What can I say, my Führer?'

Canaris intervened. 'The question of the Suez Canal. Captain Ritter has come up with an extraordinary plan. In fact, what is the most extraordinary thing about it is its simplicity.' He laid the file on Hitler's desk. 'Operation Sheba.'

Hitler leaned back, arms folded in an inimitable gesture. 'I'll read it later. Tell me, Captain Ritter.'

Ritter licked dry lips. 'Well, my Führer, it all started

with a professor of archaeology at the University called Muller and an extraordinary find he made in Southern Arabia.'

'Fascinating,' Hitler said, his eyes glowing, for his passion for architecture was intense. 'I'd give anything to see that temple.' He sat back. 'But go on, Captain. You use the site as a base, but how does that advance the cause?'

'The essence of the plan is its absurd simplicity. A single plane, a bomber trying to attack the Canal is an absurdity. One can never be certain of accuracy.'

'So?' Hitler said.

'There is a two-engined amphibian called the Catalina, an American plane that can drop wheels and land on the ground as well as water. It has an extraordinary cruising range. Better than sixteen hundred miles carrying a bomb load of one and a half thousand pounds.'

'Impressive,' Hitler said. 'And how would such a plane be used?'

'As I say, absurdly simple, my Führer. The plane lands at our site in the desert and takes on not bombs, but mines. It flies to Egypt and lands on the Suez Canal itself. There the crew offload many mines, which will drift on the current. I would suggest somewhere near Kantra as a good spot. The crew will of course sink the Catalina, leaving on board a large quantity of our latest explosive, Helicon, which will do an enormous amount of damage to the Canal itself. I need hardly point out that the mines floating down will meet ships travelling north from Lake Timsah. I think we may count on several sinking and thus causing a further blockage.'

There was silence for a while as Hitler sat there staring into space and then he smacked a fist into his palm. 'Brilliant and as you say, absurdly simple.' He frowned. 'But this plane, this Catalina. Can you get hold of one?'

'There is one available for sale in Lisbon, my Führer. I thought we could buy it and start our own airline in Dahrein, a Spanish company, naturally. I'm sure there would be plenty of coastal trade.'

Hitler got up, came round the desk and clapped him on the shoulders. 'Quite. I like this man, Herr Admiral. Put his plan into force at once. You have my full authorization.'

'My Führer.' Canaris led the way to the door, turned and forced himself to give the Nazi salute. 'Let's get out of here,' he whispered to Ritter, turned and opened the door.

As they went along the Marble Gallery Canaris said, 'You certainly covered yourself with glory there. Naturally I'll authorize the necessary funding for the Catalina but it occurs to me that there might be a problem regarding a suitable crew. Of course, there is no reason why Germans should not be flying for a Spanish airline.'

'But much better if they were Spanish,' Ritter said.

'And where would you procure them?'

'The ranks of the SS, Herr Admiral, they have many Spanish volunteers.'

'Of course,' Canaris said. 'It would be perfect.'

'I have already tracked down a suitable pilot, a man with much combat experience in the Spanish Civil War. He is at present employed as a courier pilot by the SS. I'm seeing him later this morning at Gatow airfield.'

'Good. I'll come with you and see for myself,' Canaris said, and led the way down the marble stairs.

Carlos Romero was twenty-seven; a saturnine, rather handsome young man, son of a wealthy Madrid wine merchant, he had learned to fly at sixteen, had joined the Spanish Air Force at the earliest possible moment and trained as a fighter pilot. When the Civil War came he had opted for Franco, not because he was a dedicated Fascist, but because that's what people of his class did. He'd shot down eleven planes, and had the time of his life. He'd even flown with the German Condor Legion.

Suddenly it was all over and he didn't want that, and then he'd got a whisper that the SS were taking Spanish volunteers. A pilot with his record they had snapped up without hesitation, employing him mainly on courier duties, ferrying high-ranking officers.

So here he was at the controls of a small Stork spotter plane a thousand feet above Berlin, an SS Brigadeführer behind him. He called the tower at Gatow, received permission to land and drifted down towards the airfield, bored out of his skull.

'Mother of God,' he whispered softly in Spanish, 'there must be something better than this.'

There was, of course, and he found it when he went into the mess and took off his flying jacket, revealing a well-tailored SS uniform in field grey. He had a small Spanish shield on his left shoulder, and wore the Spanish Order of Merit for gallantry in the field and an Iron Cross First Class for his exploits with the Condor Legion.

He was aware of Canaris first, because of his high rank, although he did not recognize him, but Ritter he did, and went forward with genuine pleasure.

'Hans Ritter, by all that's holy.'

Ritter got up to greet him, leaning on his stick, and shook hands. 'You look well, Carlos. Spain seems a long time ago.'

'I heard about your leg. I'm sorry.'

Ritter said, 'Admiral Canaris, Head of the Abwehr.'

Romero got his heels together and saluted. 'An honour, Herr Admiral.'

'Join us, Herr Hauptsturmführer.' Canaris waved to the mess steward. Champagne. Bollinger for preference, and three glasses.' He turned to Romero. 'You are a courier pilot, I understand. Do you like that?'

'To be frank, Herr Admiral, these milk runs of mine bore me to death.'

'Then we'll have to see if we can find something more rewarding for you,' Canaris said as the champagne arrived. 'Tell him, Hans.'

Romero finished reading the file and closed it. His face was pale and excited as he looked up. Canaris said, 'Are you interested?'

'Interested?' Romero accepted a cigarette from Ritter and his hand shook. 'Herr Admiral, I'm willing to go down on my knees and beg.'

Canaris laughed. 'No need for that.'

Ritter said, 'The Catalina would not present you with a problem?'

'Good God no, an excellent aircraft to fly.'

'And what about a crew?'

Romero sat back thinking about it. 'I could manage with a second pilot and an engineer.'

'And where would we find them?' Canaris asked.

'Right here in the Spanish Legion of the SS. Like myself, Herr Admiral. I can think of two suitable candidates right now: Javier Noval, a fine pilot, and Juan Conde, an aircraft engineer of genius.'

Ritter made a note of the names. 'Excellent. I'll have them transferred to Abwehr duties along with yourself.'

'What about the explosives and the mines?' Romero asked.

'We'll have them delivered by some suitable freighter,' Ritter told him. 'There should be no problem in a place like Dahrein. You will naturally build up your credentials during the run-up to September. Coastal trade, freight, that kind of thing.'

Romero nodded slowly. 'But I do have a suggestion. When the time comes we could make the transfer of the mines at sea. I could land beside the freighter with no problem. From there a direct flight to the base would simplify the whole thing.'

'Excellent.' Canaris stood up. 'I think you should meet our friend Professor Muller. You can come back to town with us, drop me off on the way and then continue to the University. From now on, you deal with Captain Ritter in all things.'

'At your orders. Herr Admiral.'

'Good,' Canaris said, and he turned and led the way out.

Muller's department at the University was housed in a vast echoing hall filled with artefacts of every description. Egyptian mummies, statues from Rome and Greece, amphorae retrieved from ancient wrecks at the bottom of the Mediterranean, it was all there. Ritter and Romero browsed while Muller sat at his desk in his glass office and read the Operation Sheba file. Finally he got up and went to join them.

Ritter turned. 'Well, what do you think?'

Muller was highly nervous, tried to smile and failed miserably. 'A wonderful idea, Herr Hauptman, but I wonder if I have the qualifications you need. I mean, I'm not a trained spy, I'm just an archaeologist.'

'This will be done, Professor, and by direct order of the Führer. Does this give you a problem?'

'Good heavens no.' Muller's face was ashen.

Romero clapped him on the shoulder. 'Don't worry, Professor, I'll look after you.'

Ritter said, 'That's settled then. When Hauptsturm-führer Romero leaves from Lisbon in the Catalina, you go with him, so make your preparations. I'll be in touch.'

Ritter limped away, his stick tapping the marble. As they moved along the hall to the entrance, Romero said to him, 'He's a nervous little bastard, Ritter.'

'He'll come to heel and that's all that's important.' They went out of the main entrance and stood at the top of the steps. 'I'll make arrangements for the immediate transfer of you and Noval and Conde today. You'll leave for Lisbon tomorrow, in civilian clothes naturally. I'll arrange priority seats on the Lufthansa flight. As regards the purchase of the Catalina our man at the German Legation will be your banker. Once you've checked the plane out, report back to me on the Embassy secure phone. I'll expect to hear from you by Thursday at the latest.'

'Mother of God, but you don't hang about, Hans, do you?'

'I could never see the point,' Ritter said, and started down the steps to the Mercedes.

The River Tagus, as someone once said, is the true reason for the existence of Lisbon, with its wide bays and many sheltered anchorages. It was from here that the great flying boats, the mighty clippers, left for America and it was here, attached to two buoys about three hundred yards out to sea from the waterfront, that Carlos Romero found the Catalina. He had arrived at the dock close to the Avenida da India together with Javier Noval and Juan Conde ten minutes early for the appointment with the owner's agent, a man called da Gama. They stood at the edge of the dock looking out at the amphibian.

'It looks good to me,' said Noval, a tough young man around Romero's age, who wore an old leather flying jacket.

Conde was older than either of them, thirty-five and stocky. He also wore a flying jacket and looked across at the Catalina, shading his eyes from the sun.

'What do you think, Juan, can you handle it?'

'Just try me.'

A motor boat nosed in to the dock and a man in brown suit and Panama hat waved from the stern. 'Señor Romero?' he called in Spanish. 'Fernando da Gama. Come aboard.'

They went down the steps and joined him, and he nodded to the boatman, who took the motorboat away.

'She looks good?' da Gama suggested.

'She looks bloody marvellous,' Romero told him. 'What's the story?'

'A local shipping line had the idea of regular flights down to the island of Madeira. Purchased the Catalina in the United States last year. It has performed magnificently, but they wanted to concentrate on passengers and the capacity is limited – too limited for there to be any money in it. May I ask what your requirement would be?'

Romero stayed very close to the truth. 'General freight in the Red Sea and Gulf of Aden, flying as far as Goa perhaps. It's a new venture.'

'I know that area,' da Gama said. 'The Catalina would be perfect.'

They bumped alongside a small floating dock and as the boatman killed his motor, Noval and Conde grabbed a line and tied up. Da Gama opened the cabin door and led the way in. Romero looked into the cockpit with conscious pleasure, took one of the pilot's seats and reached for the control column. Noval took the other seat and examined the instrument panel.

'What a beauty.'

Da Gama, Conde at his shoulder, opened a file. 'I'll just give you approximate dimensions. Length sixty-three feet, height twenty, wingspan a hundred and four. The twin engines are Pratt and Whitney, twelve hundred horsepower each. Cruising speed a hundred and eighty miles an hour. Remarkably long range. Without freight it is possible to fly for four thousand miles before the need to refuel. I can't think of another aircraft that could do this.'

'Neither can I,' Romero told him and got up. 'You can take us back now.'

As they scrambled into the motor boat da Gama tried the usual tack. 'Of course, a number of people are interested.'

The motor boat pulled away and Romero said, 'Drop the sales pitch, my friend, just draw up the contract. I'll give you my lawyer's name, we sign tomorrow and you'll receive a cheque for your asking price. Satisfied?'

Da Gama looked astonished. 'But of course, Señor.'

Romero took out a cigarette and accepted a light from Noval. He looked back at the Catalina and blew out a long plume of smoke.

'Looks like we're in business, boys,' he said.

★

Baron Oswald von Hoyningen-Heune was Minister to the German Legation in Lisbon. An aristocrat and career diplomat of the old school, he was no Nazi and, like most of his staff, was thankful to be as far away from Berlin as possible. Initially wary of the strange Spaniard who was a Hauptsturmführer in the SS, and resigned to following orders from Berlin, he had been pleasantly surprised, had taken to Romero.

He rose to greet him now as the Spaniard entered his office. 'My dear Romero, it went well?'

'Couldn't have been better. Da Gama will be in touch with the lawyer you gave me. You provide the funding and we conclude tomorrow. I'll need to speak to Captain Ritter at Abwehr Headquarters at once, by the way.'

'Of course.' The Baron reached for the red secure phone on his desk and placed the call. 'It shouldn't take long.' He stood up. 'Cognac?'

'Why not?'

Romero lit a cigarette and sat on one of the sofas. The baron handed him a glass and sat opposite. 'All very intriguing, this business.'

'And also highly secret.'

'But of course. I'm not prying. In fact, I'd rather not know.' He raised his glass. 'But I'll drink to your success anyway.'

At that moment the red phone rang. Romero said, 'With your permission?'

'But of course. I'll leave you to it.'

The Baron went out and Romero picked up the phone. 'Hans, is that you?'

'Who else?' Ritter said. 'How did it go?'

'Perfect,' Romero told him. 'A superb aircraft. I couldn't be more pleased. Tell the Admiral we're on our way.'

Ritter knocked on the door and went in. Canaris was drinking tea, one of the dachshunds on his lap. He looked up.

'What is it, Hans?'

'Romero has just spoken to me from Lisbon, Herr Admiral. The Catalina is perfect and the sale will be concluded tomorrow.'

'Excellent.' Canaris nodded. 'Do an additional report bringing everything up to date and I'll make an appointment for us to see the Führer.'

'At once, Herr Admiral.'

As Ritter limped to the door, Canaris called, 'Oh, and Hans.'

'Yes, Herr Admiral?'

'We'll take Muller with us.'

The summons came sooner than they had expected and took them to the Chancellery for an appointment at ten o'clock that night. They picked up Muller at the University on the way and the news that he was to meet the Führer shocked him completely.

When they reached the reception area of Hitler's suite the aide on duty rose to greet them. 'I understand you have a report for the Führer, Herr Admiral.'

'That's right,' Canaris said.

The aide held out his hand. 'He would like to read it before seeing you.'

'Of course.'

Canaris gave him the file; the aide opened the door and went in. Canaris nodded to the other two and they sat down.

Muller was trembling slightly and Canaris said, 'Are you all right?'

'For God's sake, how do you expect me to feel, Admiral. This is the Führer we're talking about. What do I say?'

'As little as possible,' Canaris told him and added with some irony, 'Remember he's a great man and behave accordingly.'

The door opened and the aide appeared. 'Gentlemen, our Führer will see you now.'

The room was a place of shadows, and Hitler sat at the enormous desk with only the light of a single brass lamp. He was reading the file, closed it and looked up.

'Still brilliant, Herr Admiral. An absolutely first-class job.'

'Captain Ritter really deserves all the credit.'

'No, Herr Admiral, I think after all this that *Major* Ritter would be more appropriate. In fact, I warn you that I could well steal him for my own staff.'

He stood up and Ritter said the obvious thing. 'You do me too much honour, my Führer.'

Hitler came round the corner of his desk and approached Muller. 'Professor Muller, isn't it? An amazing discovery and you sacrifice it for the sake of the Reich.'

And Muller, shaking almost uncontrollably, said exactly the right thing. 'For you, my Führer, for you.'

Hitler clapped him on the shoulders. 'A great day is coming, gentlemen, the greatest in Germany's history.' He walked slowly away and the desk lamp threw his shadow across the huge map of the world. He stood there, arms folded. 'You may go, gentlemen.'

Canaris nodded to the other two, jerked his head and led the way out.

Later, after dropping Muller off at the University, Canaris told the driver to take them back to Tirpitz Ufer. As they turned into a side street they came to a café on the corner, windows lighted.

Canaris leaned forward. 'Stop here.' He turned to

34

Ritter. 'A nightcap, coffee and schnapps. We'll toast your promotion, Major.'

'My pleasure, Herr Admiral.'

The café was almost deserted and the proprietor was overwhelmed. He ushered them to a booth by the window and hurriedly took the order. Canaris pulled out his cigarette case and proffered it to Ritter, who took one and gave him a light.

'He was pleased,' the Admiral said and blew out smoke. 'Muller was a mess though. He's not strong enough.'

'I agree,' Ritter said. 'We need a professional to back him up.'

The proprietor brought coffee and schnapps on a tray and Canaris waved him away. 'You'll have to find somebody, an old Abwehr hand. Somebody reliable.'

'No problem, Herr Admiral.'

'You know this thing is so simple it could work,' Canaris said and poured schnapps from the bottle into two glasses.

'I agree,' Ritter said.

Canaris nodded. 'There's only one problem.'

'And what's that, Herr Admiral?'

'It won't win us this coming war, my friend, nothing can do that. You see, Hans, we're all going straight to hell, but here's to your promotion anyway.'

He raised the glass of schnapps and drained it at a single swallow.

DAHREIN

....

August 1939

THREE

THE WIND, BLOWING across the Gulf from Africa, still carried some of the warmth of the day to Kane as he stood on the deck of the launch, listening.

There was no moon and yet the sky seemed to be alive, to glow with the incandescence of millions of stars. He breathed deeply, inhaling the freshness, and followed a school of flying-fish with his eyes as they curved out of the sea in a shower of phosphorescent water.

A door opened and light from the saloon momentarily flooded out as Piroo, the Hindu deck-hand, came up the companionway with a mug of steaming coffee.

Kane sipped some of it gratefully. 'That's good.'

'The *Kantara* is late tonight, Sahib,' Piroo said.

Kane nodded and checked his watch. 'Almost two a.m. I wonder what the old devil O'Hara is playing at?'

'Perhaps it's the whisky again.'

Kane grinned. 'More than likely.'

As he finished his coffee, Piroo touched him on the arm. 'I think she comes, Sahib.'

Kane listened intently. At first he was conscious only of the slap of the waves against the hull of the launch and the whisper of the wind, and then he became aware of a muffled, gentle throbbing across the water. In the distance, he saw the green pin-point of light that was the starboard navigation light of the *Kantara*.

'Not before time,' he said softly.

He went into the wheelhouse and switched on the navigation lights, and when he pressed the starter, the engine coughed into life. He waited until the steamer was almost upon them, before he opened the throttle gently and took the launch forward on a course which would bring them together.

The old freighter was doing no more than two or three knots, and Piroo put out the fenders as Kane took the launch in close. A Lascar appeared at the rail and tossed down a line which Piroo quickly secured. A rope ladder followed a moment later, and Kane cut the engines and went out on deck.

The high, rust-streaked side of the *Kantara* reared into the night, the single stack a long black shadow above. As he climbed the ladder, Kane wondered, and not for the first time, exactly what it was that kept this heap of scrap-iron floating.

He scrambled over the rail and said in Hindi, 'Where's the Captain?'

The Lascar shrugged. 'In his cabin.'

He quickly climbed a companionway to the upper deck and knocked on the door of the captain's cabin. There was no reply. After a moment, he opened it and went in. The cabin was in darkness and the stench was appalling. He fumbled for the light switch and turned it on.

O'Hara was on his bunk. He lay on his back in singlet and pants, mouth open, exposing decaying yellow teeth. Empty whisky bottles rolled across the floor with the motion of the ship, and Kane wrinkled his nose in disgust and went out on deck.

Another Lascar was waiting for him. 'The mate, he say you go to bridge,' the man said.

Kane crossed the deck quickly and climbed an iron ladder to the bridge. Guptas, the mate, was at the wheel, his turbaned head disembodied in the light from the binnacle.

Kane leaned in the doorway and lit a cigarette. 'How long has he been like that?'

Guptas grinned. 'Ever since we left Aden. It should take him at least two days to sleep this one off.'

'What a way to run a ship,' Kane said. 'What happened this time, anyway? Why didn't you call at Dahrein on the run-in from Bombay, as usual?'

'We had cargo for Mombasa,' Guptas told him. 'After that, Aden.'

'Skiros wasn't too pleased,' Kane said. 'I presume you've got the stuff all right.'

Guptas nodded. 'They should be bringing it up now. By the way, we have a passenger this trip.'

'A passenger?' Kane said incredulously. 'On this tub?'

'An American woman,' Guptas said. 'She wanted to leave Aden in a hurry. We were the only ship available and the Catalina wasn't due for a week.'

Kane flicked his cigarette in a glowing spiral into the night.

'Then I won't hang about. No sense in waking her up. She might get curious.'

Guptas nodded in agreement. 'I think that would be wise. A strange thing happened just before dawn yesterday.'

'What was that?'

'The Catalina – Romero's Catalina. We saw it on the horizon about thirty miles out. It landed beside some Portuguese freighter. They were offloading crates.'

'So what's the difference between that and what we're doing now? So Romero's doing a little smuggling too.' Kane shrugged. 'We've all got to get by. I'll see you next month.' And he went down the ladder to the deck.

He leaned over the rail and watched two Lascars lower an oil drum down to Piroo on the deck of the launch. A voice said quietly from behind, 'Do you happen to have a light?'

He turned quickly. She was rather tall and the smooth rounded face might have suggested weakness had it not been for the firm mouth. She wore a scarf and a light duster coat.

He held out a match in his cupped hands. 'Rather late for a promenade round the deck.'

She blew smoke out and leaned against the rail. 'I couldn't sleep. The facilities for passengers on this ship are strictly limited.'

'That I can believe.'

'A strange place to meet a fellow–American.'

He grinned. 'We pop up everywhere these days.'

She leaned over the rail and looked down at the launch. 'That's your boat, I presume?'

He nodded. 'I'm a deep–sea fisherman out of Dahrein. Got caught in a storm and ran out of fuel. It's lucky the *Kantara* came along.'

'I suppose it is,' she said.

Her perfume hung disturbingly in the air and, for some reason, he could think of nothing more to say. And then Piroo hailed him from the launch and he smiled. 'I'll have to be going.'

'Ships that pass in the night,' she said.

He went down the ladder quickly and Piroo cast off the line. The *Kantara* pulled away from them at once and, when he looked up, he could see the woman in the yellow glare of the deck lights, leaning over the rail watching them until they faded into the night.

He dismissed her from his mind for the moment, because there were more important things to think of. The two-gallon oil can stood on the deck where Piroo had left it. Kane checked it quickly and then went below to the saloon.

Piroo had the air tank ready, and Kane stripped to his shorts and the Hindu helped him on with it. They went up on deck. Piroo vanished into the wheelhouse and emerged with a large, powerful spot-lamp on a long cable, specially designed for underwater use, which plugged into the boat's lighting system.

A ring bolt had been welded to each end of the oil can, and Piroo threaded a manilla rope through them as Kane pulled on his diving mask and gripped the mouth-piece of his breathing tube firmly between his teeth. He took the lamp in one hand and vaulted over the side.

For a moment, he paused to adjust the flow of oxygen and then he swam down in a long, sweeping curve that brought him underneath the hull.

The sensation of being alone in a silent world, of floating in space, was somehow accentuated by the circumstances. The water gleamed with a sort of phosphorescent fire all around him, and transparent fish, attracted by the lamp, glowed in its light.

After a moment, the oil can dropped down through the water. He grabbed the manilla rope with one hand and quickly passed it through two more ring bolts set in the keel of the launch.

He turned from securing it and paused, held by the wonder of the scene. The sea seemed alive with fish, incandescent, glowing like candles in its depths. A school of barracuda flashed by like silver streaks, and then an eight-foot shark swung into the beam of the lamp and poised there, watching him.

As it moved forward, he pulled his breathing tube from his mouth, emitting a stream of silvery bubbles. The shark altered course with a flick of its tail and disappeared into the gloom.

He swam up to the surface quickly and Piroo pulled him up over the low rail. 'Everything all right, Sahib?'

Kane nodded as he unstrapped the tank. 'No trouble at all. One shark, and he was only trying to be playful.'

The Hindu grinned, teeth flashing in the darkness, and handed him a towel, and Kane went below. The water had been surprisingly cold, and he rubbed himself down briskly and then dressed.

When he went back on deck, the wind was freshening and Piroo brought him more coffee. As he drank it, Kane caught a last glimpse of the *Kantara*'s navigation lights on the horizon, and remembered the woman.

She had certainly been attractive and he wondered

what she was doing on an old tub like the *Kantara*. There could be no satisfactory answer, of course.

For a moment, he seemed to catch a faint touch of her perfume on the night air. He smiled wryly and, going into the wheelhouse, started the engines and took the launch forward into the night.

FOUR

THEY CAME INTO DAHREIN in the early afternoon. As the launch rounded the curved promontory crowded with its white houses, a two-masted dhow, lateen sails bellying in the Gulf breeze, moved out of harbour on the long haul across the Arabian Sea to India.

The *Kantara* was unloading at the jetty. On the white curve of the beach, fishermen sat patiently mending their nets and a few children played naked in the shallows.

Kane cut the engines and signalled to Piroo, who was standing in the stern, anchor ready in his hands. It disappeared into the green waters of the harbour with a splash. For a moment longer, the launch glided forward and then, with a gentle tug, it came to a halt fifty or sixty yards from the crumbling stone jetty that formed the east side of the harbour.

Piroo disappeared into the cabin, and Kane stepped out of the wheelhouse. He lit a cigarette and walked slowly along to the stern, where he stood with one foot on the brass rail, the peak of his battered and salt-stained cap pulled well forward to shield his eyes from the intense glare of the sun.

He was a tall, powerful man in faded blue denims and sweat-shirt. His brown hair was bleached by the sun and badly needed cutting, and there was a three days' growth of beard on his chin. The sun-dried skin of his face was drawn tightly over prominent cheek-bones and his eyes were deep-set in their sockets, calm and expressionless, always staring into the middle distance or beyond the next hill as if perpetually searching for something.

As he looked across the harbour, a small rowing boat appeared from between two moored dhows. The brawny Arab who pulled on the oars was being urged on by a fat, bearded official in crumpled khaki uniform and white head-cloth. There was a slight cough from behind, and Kane reached out a hand without turning round. Piroo passed him a large gin-sling in which ice tinkled, and said gently, 'Perhaps Captain González will wish to search the boat, Sahib?'

Kane shrugged. 'That's what he's paid for.'

He sipped the drink slowly, savouring its coldness with conscious pleasure, and watched the boat approach. As it bumped against the side of the launch González smiled up at him, his face shiny with sweat, a paper

Japanese fan fluttering in his right hand in a vain effort to keep the flies at bay.

Kane grinned down at him. 'Looks as if the heat's getting to you, Juan.'

González shrugged, and replied in perfect English, 'Only duty compelled me to put in an appearance on the quay in my official capacity when the mail boat came in from Aden.' He mopped his face with a corner of his head-cloth. 'Where are you from this time?'

Kane finished his drink and handed the glass to Piroo, who was still standing at his elbow. 'Mukalla,' he said. 'I had some letters to deliver for Marie Perret.'

González kissed his fingers. 'Ah, the delightful Mademoiselle Perret. We are privileged men. Here on earth a glimpse of Paradise. Are you carrying any cargo?'

Kane shook his head. 'We tried for a shark on the way back, but he took half my line as well as the hook.'

González raised a hand and rolled his eyes. 'You Americans – so energetic, and for what?'

'Are you coming aboard to check?' Kane said.

González shook his head. 'Would I insult a friend?' He waved to the oarsman to push off. 'I hurry home to a tall drink and the cool hand of my wife.'

Kane watched the boat disappear amongst the mass of moored fishing dhows that floated a few yards from the beach. After a while, he tossed his cigarette down into the water and turned from the rail. 'I think I'll go for a swim,' he said. 'Get the deck swabbed down, Piroo. Afterwards, you can go ashore to visit that girl of yours.'

He went below to the cabin and changed quickly. When he came back on deck, he was wearing an old pair of khaki shorts, and a cork-handled knife in leather sheath swung from the belt at his waist.

Piroo was standing by the rail, hauling vigorously on a rope, and a moment later a large canvas bucket appeared. He emptied its contents over the deck and threw it back into the water.

Kane didn't bother with a diving mask. He went past Piroo on the run and dived cleanly over the rail. At this point, the harbour was some twenty feet deep, and he swam down through the clear green water, revelling in its coolness. For a brief moment he hovered over the bottom, and then he kicked against the white sand and started up.

When he had almost reached the surface, he changed direction slightly until he was underneath the hull. The two-gallon oil can still hung suspended beneath the keel as he had left it.

He examined it and then quickly surfaced. Piroo was standing at the rail, the canvas bucket in his hands. Kane nodded briefly, took a deep breath, and dived again.

When he reached the oil can, he took out his knife and slashed the rope which secured it in place. At that moment the canvas bucket bumped against his back and he pulled it towards him with his free hand and pushed the oil can inside. He jerked twice on the rope and the bucket was hoisted smoothly to the surface.

He was in no hurry. He swam down to the white sand of the harbour bottom again and then floated lazily upwards in a stream of sparkling bubbles. When he surfaced and hauled himself over the rail, the deck was deserted. A towel was lying on top of the hatch, neatly folded and waiting for him. He quickly dried his body and, as he went below, he was rubbing his damp hair briskly.

Piroo was squatting on the floor of the cabin. The oil can was between his knees and he expertly prised open the lid with a chisel. His hand disappeared inside and came out holding a bulky, oilskin package. He raised his face enquiringly. 'Shall I open, Sahib?'

Kane shook his head. 'We'll let Skiros have that pleasure. After all, he's paying. Better get rid of that can, though.'

The Hindu took the can and went up on deck. Kane hefted the package in his hands for a second, a slight frown on his face, then he dropped it on to the table and went and lay on the bunk.

Tiredness flooded through him in a sudden wave and he remembered that he hadn't slept for the past twenty-four hours. He closed his eyes and relaxed. There was the unmistakable bump of a boat against the side of the launch, and Piroo appeared in the doorway. 'It is Selim, Sahib.'

For a moment Kane sat on the edge of the bunk, a frown on his face, and then he slipped a hand under the pillow and took out a .45-calibre Colt automatic. He pushed it into the waistband of his pants, brushed past Piroo, and went up on deck.

A tall Arab was climbing over the rail. He was dressed in immaculate white robes, and his head-cloth was bound with cords of black silk. Cold eyes flashed in a swarthy face and his mouth was thin and twisted by an old scar, which disappeared into the beard.

'What the hell do you want?' Kane demanded.

Selim fingered the silver haft of the curved *jambiya* at his belt. 'Skiros sent me,' he said. 'I have come for the package.'

'Then you can bloody well go back to Skiros and tell him to come himself,' Kane said. 'I'm particular who I have on my boat.'

'One day you will go too far,' Selim said softly. 'One day I may have to kill you.'

'I'm frightened to death.'

The Arab controlled his anger with difficulty. 'The package.'

Kane pulled the Colt from his waistband and cocked it. 'Get off my boat.'

In the sudden dangerous silence which followed, a cask boomed hollowly from across the harbour as a labourer rolled it along the wharf. Selim's hand tightened over the hilt of his *jambiya*, and Kane took a quick pace forward, lifted a foot and pushed him back over the low rail.

The two Arab seamen who were sitting at the oars of the heavy rowing boat hastily pulled their master over the stern, where he sprawled for a moment, coughing up water, sodden robes clinging to his body.

Kane stood with a foot on the rail, the Colt held negligently in one hand. For a moment Selim glared up at him and then he snapped his fingers and the two oarsmen pushed off from the launch, faces expressionless.

On the other side of the rusty freighter at the jetty, a large, three-masted dhow was moored, which Kane recognized as Selim's boat, the *Farah*. The rowing boat moved slowly towards it and, after watching for a few moments, he turned from the rail.

Piroo shook his head slowly and his face was troubled. 'That was a bad thing to do, Sahib. Selim will not forget.'

Kane shrugged. 'Let me worry about that.' He yawned lazily as the tiredness took hold of him again. 'I think I'll sleep for a while. Let me know when Skiros turns up.'

Piroo nodded obediently and squatted on the deck, his back against the rail, as Kane went below.

He pushed the Colt back under the pillow, poured himself a drink, and then lit a cigarette and went to the bunk. He lay with his head against the pillow, staring at the roof of the cabin, watching the blue smoke twist and swirl in the current from the air conditioner, and thought about Selim.

He was well known in every port from the Red Sea to the Persian Gulf. He traded in anything that would make him a profit — gold, arms, even human beings. That was the part of his activities which Kane couldn't stomach. There was still a heavy demand for slaves, particularly female, in most Arab countries. Selim did his best to satisfy that demand. His speciality was young girls.

Kane wondered how Selim would react if the *Farah* happened to meet with an accident one dark night. It could be simply arranged. A charge of that plastic waterproof explosive he had used on the salvage job at Mukalla would do the trick. It was a pleasant thought.

His eyes closed and the darkness moved in on him.

He had slept for no more than an hour when a gentle pressure on his shoulder caused him to awaken. Piroo was standing by the bunk.

Kane pushed himself up on one elbow. 'What is it — Skiros?'

The Hindu nodded gravely. 'He is waiting on the jetty, Sahib.'

Kane swung his legs to the floor, stood up and stretched. 'Okay, you'd better bring him across in the dinghy.'

He went up on deck, the Hindu at his heels. Skiros was standing on the edge of the jetty, his face shaded by a large Panama hat. He was wearing a soiled white linen suit, and a slight breeze lifted from the water against him, moulding his grotesque figure.

As Piroo dropped down into the dinghy and sculled rapidly towards him, the Greek raised his malacca cane and called cheerfully, 'Is it safe for me to come across? I've already had one bath today.'

Kane waved a hand. 'I'll have a drink waiting for you.'

He watched Skiros negotiate the iron ladder pinned to the side of the jetty and safely step into the dinghy, and then he went below. He had just finished mixing two gin-slings when the dinghy bumped against the hull of the launch. A moment later Skiros creaked heavily down the stairs and entered the cabin.

He flopped into a chair with a groan. 'Why the hell do you have to anchor your boat in the middle of the harbour? Why can't you tie up at one of the jetties like everybody else?'

Sweat stained his jacket in great patches and trickled

along the folds of his fat face. He produced a red silk handkerchief and mopped the worst of it away, then removed his Panama and proceeded to fan himself. His hair was shiny with pomade and carefully combed, and his tiny black eyes sparkled with cunning.

Kane handed him one of the drinks. 'You should know me by now. I don't trust anybody in this damned town. Let's say I prefer to have a moat around me.'

Skiros shook his head. 'Crazy Americans. I shall never understand you.' He sipped appreciatively at his drink and then placed it carefully on the table. 'I believe you had a little trouble with Selim?'

Kane lit a cigarette. 'I wouldn't call it trouble. I simply tossed him off my boat. Since when has he been working for you, anyway?'

The Greek shrugged, and took his time over lighting an oily black cheroot. 'I find him useful, now and then. He does the odd trip to India for me when it's necessary. I only sent him this afternoon because I was busy with something else.'

Kane frowned. 'Well, don't send him again. I don't like his smell. I once picked up four slaves he dumped overboard three miles out in the Gulf when a British gunboat was on his heels.'

Skiros shrugged and raised one hand in a gesture of submission. 'All right, so you don't like the way he makes his money, but take a tip from me. He's lost a lot of face over the way you treated him this afternoon. From now on I'd be extremely careful if I were you.'

Kane pushed the oilskin package across the table. 'Let's get down to business.'

Skiros produced a clasp knife and proceeded to cut open the package carefully. 'Did you have any trouble?'

Kane shook his head. 'I was at the rendezvous just after midnight. The boat was late, and O'Hara was drunk as usual. Guptas was in charge. He told me something interesting.'

'What was that?'

'They saw the Catalina about thirty miles out, off-loading from a Portuguese freighter.'

Skiros laughed. 'So Romero's developed sticky fingers too. That *is* interesting. What about customs when you came in?'

Kane shrugged. 'No trouble there. Gonzalez didn't even come on board. All that business with the oil can under the keel was a waste of time.'

Skiros shook his head. 'Nothing is a waste of time in this work. One day, when you least expect it, he will take it into his head to perform his duties conscientiously.' He removed the outer wrappings of the package as he spoke, and revealed a neat stack of Indian rupees.

As Skiros counted the bundles, Kane shook his head. 'I'll never understand this racket. Gold smuggled *into* India, rupees smuggled *out*.'

Skiros smiled. 'It's all a question of exchange. In this modern world it is really so easy to make money. One doesn't need to steal at all.' His face was shiny with sweat once more. He held his hands lightly over the stack of bank-notes and sighed. 'Ah, my friend, if you knew the effect money has on me. When I moved here from Goa six months ago I'd no idea what a gold mine the place is.'

Kane poured himself another drink. 'Why don't you try spending some of it once in a while?'

Skiros shrugged. 'I started life on a mountain farm in northern Greece. The fields were more stones than soil. My mother was an old woman at twenty-five, and one year, when the crops failed in the drought, my two sisters died of starvation. It is something I have never forgotten. That is why I live only to make money. I gloat over the size of my bank balance. I begrudge every penny I have to pay out.'

Kane grinned. 'While we're on the subject of paying out, I'll take my cut now. Dollars as usual, if you don't mind.'

Skiros laughed so that the flesh trembled on his huge body. 'But I would never forget you, my friend. After all, you are an essential part of my whole organization. The king-pin, I believe you call it.'

'Skip the flattery and let's have the cash,' Kane said.

Skiros produced a bulging wallet and proceeded to

count out hundred-dollar bills. His hands were sweating, and he placed each bill reluctantly upon the table. When he had reached twenty, he paused, then added five more. 'There you are, my friend,' he said. 'We agreed on two thousand, but I give you a bonus of five hundred dollars. Let no man say Skiros does not reward good service.'

Kane swept the bills into the table drawer. 'You old spider. You know damned well, most of it will come back to you, either over the bar at your hotel or across the gambling tables.'

Skiros laughed again, his face crinkling so that the eyes almost disappeared, and pushed himself to his feet. 'Now I must go.' He moved to the door and then paused. 'But I am forgetting some important news.' He turned slowly. 'A woman came in from Aden on the boat this afternoon. An American named Cunningham – Mrs Ruth Cunningham. Extremely pretty. She has been asking for you.'

Kane stiffened, a surprised frown crossing his face. 'I don't know anyone called Cunningham.'

Skiros shrugged. 'She appears to know you, or to know *of* you at least. She is staying at my hotel. I told her I would be seeing you, and she asked me to give you a message. She would like you to come to the hotel. She said it was most important.'

Kane still frowned down at the table, leaning forward,

his weight on his hands. After a slight pause Skiros said, 'You will come?'

Kane straightened up and nodded. 'Sure, I'll come. I'll be there some time this evening.'

Skiros nodded. 'Good, I shall tell her.' He smiled. 'Don't look so worried. Perhaps she is only a tourist. Maybe she wishes to charter your boat to go spear-fishing along the reef.'

Kane nodded slowly. 'Yes, you're probably right.' But he didn't believe that was the reason – not for a moment – and, after Skiros had gone, he went back to the bunk and lay staring at the ceiling, groping back into the past, trying to place Ruth Cunningham. But it was no good. The name meant nothing to him.

He glanced at his watch. It was just after three, and for a little while longer he lay there; then, with a sigh of exasperation, he swung his legs to the floor and started to dress.

He pulled on his faded denims and a sweat-shirt and went up on deck. Piroo was lounging against the rail, head bowed against his chest so that only the top of his white turban was visible. Kane stirred him slightly with one foot, and the Hindu came awake at once and rose easily to his feet. 'I'm going ashore,' Kane said. 'What about you?'

Piroo shrugged. 'I think not, Sahib. Later, perhaps. I will row you across to the jetty and then return with the dinghy. It would be wiser. Selim might return.'

Kane nodded. 'Maybe you've got a point. If he does, you'll find my Colt underneath the pillow. Don't hesitate to use it. I've got more friends round here than he has.'

He dropped over the side into the dinghy, and Piroo took the oars and pulled rapidly towards the crumbling stone jetty. When they reached it, Kane stepped on to the iron ladder and climbed it quickly. As his eyes drew level with the top of the jetty, he saw a woman sitting on a large stone a few feet away, watching him.

He moved forward and she got to her feet and came to meet him. She was dressed in an expensive white linen dress, a blue silk scarf was bound round her head, peasant-fashion, and she wore sunglasses.

When she removed them, he recognized her at once as the woman he had met on the *Kantara* the previous night.

She smiled uncertainly, and there was puzzlement in her voice. 'You again! But I was looking for Captain Kane – Captain Gavin Kane.'

'That's me,' he said. 'You'll be Mrs Cunningham. What can I do for you?'

She frowned and shook her head in bewilderment. 'Mr Andrews, the American Consul in Aden, advised me to look you up. He told me you were an archaeologist. That you were an expert on Southern Arabia.'

He smiled slightly. 'I presume, you mean I don't look the part. Andrews was right on both counts. I am an archaeologist among other things, and I *do* know something about Southern Arabia. In what way can I help you?'

She stared out over the harbour, a slight frown on her face, and then she turned and looked at him coolly from steady grey eyes. 'I want you to find my husband, and I'm willing to pay highly for your services.'

He reached for a cigarette and lit it slowly. 'How high?'

She shrugged and said calmly. 'Five thousand dollars now and another five when, and if, you find him.'

For several moments they stood looking at each other and then he sighed. 'Let's discuss this over a cold drink. I know just the place.' And he took her arm, and they went along the jetty to the waterfront.

FIVE

THEY DIDN'T TALK much on the way to the hotel. Ruth Cunningham replaced her sunglasses and gazed about her with obvious interest, and Kane employed the time in studying her.

As they turned off the jetty and moved along the waterfront, he decided that Skiros had been wrong. She was not pretty – she was beautiful. The long slim lines of her were revealed to perfection by the simple linen dress as she walked. It had been a long time since he had talked to a woman like her – to a woman of his own kind.

The hotel was a tall, slender building with a crumbling façade and one narrow entrance that fronted on to the street. Inside, an ancient fan slowly revolved in the stifling heat, and he led the way across the entrance hall and into the bar.

There was no one there and the french windows which gave access to the terrace outside, creaked in the slight breeze from the harbour. Ruth Cunningham removed her sun glasses and frowned.

'Isn't there any service in this place?'

Kane shrugged. 'There isn't a great deal of action around here. Most people sleep during the afternoon. They figure it's too hot to do anything else.'

She smiled. 'Well, they say travel broadens the mind.'

He went behind the bar. 'Why don't you go and sit on the terrace while I get you a drink? There's a wind coming in from the sea. You might find it a little cooler.'

She nodded, walked out through the french windows and sat down in a large cane chair shaded by a gaudy umbrella. Kane opened the ancient icebox that stood under the bar and took out two large bottles of lager, so cold the moisture had frosted on the outside. He knocked off the caps on the edge of the zinc-topped bar, poured the contents into two tall, thin glasses and went out to the terrace.

She smiled up at him gratefully when he handed her the glass, and quickly swallowed some of the beer. She sighed. 'I'd forgotten anything could be so cold. This place is like a furnace. Frankly, I can't imagine anyone living here from choice.'

He offered her a cigarette. 'Oh, it has its points.'

She smiled slightly. 'I'm afraid they've escaped me so far.'

She leaned back against the faded cushions of her chair. 'Mr Andrews told me you were from New York. That you were a lecturer in archaeology at Columbia.'

He nodded. 'That was a long time ago.'

She said casually, 'Are you married?'

He shrugged. 'Divorced. My wife and I never hit it off.'

Ruth Cunningham flushed. 'I'm sorry I brought it up. I hope I haven't upset you?'

'On the contrary,' he said. 'We all make mistakes. My wife's was in assuming that university professors are well paid.'

'And yours?'

'Mine lay in imagining I could be content with the ordered calm of academic life. I'd only stuck it for Lillian's sake. She set me free in more ways than one.'

'And so you came East?'

'Not at first. The Air Corps was offering a full-time flying course for one year, then four on the reserve. I did that. Trained as a regular pilot. It was after that I came out here. I was in Jordan with an American expedition six years ago, then I did some work for the Egyptian government, but it didn't last long. I came to Dahrein with a German geologist who needed someone who could speak Arabic. When he left, I stayed.'

'Don't you ever feel like going back home?'

'To what?' he said. 'An assistant-professorship trying

to teach ancient history to students who don't want to know?'

'Has Dahrein anything better to offer?'

He nodded. 'There's something about the place that gets into your bones. This was once Arabia Felix – Happy Arabia. It was one of the most prosperous countries in the ancient world because the spice route from India to the Mediterranean passed through here. Now it's just a barren waste, but up there in the hills, and north into the Yemen, is the last great treasure hoard for the archaeologist. City after city, some standing in ruins – like Marib, where the Queen of Sheba probably lived – others buried beneath the sand of centuries.'

'So archaeology is still your first love,' she said.

'Very much so, but we didn't come here to talk about me, Mrs Cunningham. Isn't it time we got on to the subject of your husband?'

She took a slim gold case from her purse, selected a cigarette and tapped it thoughtfully against her thumbnail. 'It's difficult to know where to begin.' She laughed ruefully. 'I suppose I was always rather spoilt.'

Kane nodded. 'It sounds possible. What about your husband?'

She frowned. 'I met John Cunningham back home at some function or other. He was an Englishman from the School of Oriental Studies in London, lecturing at Harvard for a year. We got married.'

Kane raised his eyebrows. 'Just like that?'

She nodded. 'He was tall and distinguished and very English. I'd never met anything quite like him before.'

'And when did the trouble start?'

She smiled slightly. 'You're very perceptive, Captain Kane.' For a few moments she stared down into her glass. 'To be perfectly honest, almost straight away. I soon discovered that I'd married a man of strong principles, who believed in standing on his own two feet.'

'That sounds reasonable enough.'

She shook her head and sighed. 'Not to my father. He wanted him to join the firm, and John wouldn't hear of it.'

Kane grinned. 'Well, bully for John. What happened after that?'

She leaned back in her chair. 'We lived in London. John had a research job at the University. Of course it didn't pay very much, but my father had given me a generous allowance.'

'To enable you to live in the style to which you were accustomed?' he said, and there was something suspiciously close to amusement in his voice.

She flushed slightly. 'That was the general idea.'

'And your husband didn't like it?'

She got to her feet, walked to the parapet and looked out across the harbour. 'No, he didn't like it one little bit.' Her voice was flat and colourless, and when she turned to face him, he realized she was very near to tears. 'He accepted the arrangement because he loved me.'

She came back to the table and sank down into her chair. Kane gently placed his hand on hers. 'Would you care for another drink?' She shook her head slightly and he shrugged and leaned back in his chair.

She pushed a tendril of hair back into place with one hand in a quick, graceful gesture and continued, 'You see, my father was a self-made man. He had to fight every inch of the way and he told John pretty plainly that he didn't think much of him.'

'And how did that affect your husband?'

She shrugged. 'I insisted on living in the way I'd been used to, and it took my own money to do it. John began to feel inadequate. Gradually he withdrew into himself. He spent more and more time at the University on his research. I think, in some crazy kind of way, he hoped he might make a name for himself.'

Kane sighed. 'That makes sense. And then he walked out on you, I suppose?'

She nodded. 'He didn't come home from the University one night. He left a letter for me in his office. He told me not to worry. Something very important had come up and he had to go away for a few weeks.'

'It still doesn't explain why you're looking for him here in Dahrein.'

'I'm coming to that,' she said. 'I received a package four days ago from the British Consul in Aden. It contained some documents and a letter from John. In it he said that he was leaving on the coastal steamer for Dahrein. From here he intended to go up-country to Shabwa. He'd left the package with the Consul with strict instructions to forward it to me if he hadn't claimed it himself within two months.'

Kane stared at her in complete surprise. 'But Shabwa's a bad-security area,' he said. 'Right on the edge of the Empty Quarter – one of the greatest deserts on the face of the earth. What on earth was he doing up there?'

For a moment she hesitated, and then said slowly, 'Have you ever heard of Asthar, Captain Kane?'

He frowned slightly. 'An ancient Arabian goddess – the equivalent of Venus. She was worshipped in the time of the Queen of Sheba.'

She nodded. 'That's right. The Queen of Sheba was also high priestess of the cult.' There was a moment of stillness between them before she continued in a calm voice, 'My husband had reason to believe that out there in the Empty Quarter are the ruins of the great temple Sheba built in honour of the goddess Asthar.'

For a little while there was silence as Kane looked at her in astonishment and then he shook his head. 'Oh, no, Mrs Cunningham. If that's what your husband was looking for, it's no wonder you haven't heard from him.

There isn't a damned thing out there except sand, heat and thirst.'

'My husband knew differently. You see, he made an amazing discovery some months ago. Part of his research work entailed the translation of ancient Arabic manuscripts and parchments, many of which had come from St Catherine's Monastery on Mount Sinai. While working on one of these, he noticed it had been used before and the older script partially erased. By using specialized equipment available at the University, he managed to make a copy of the original writing.'

Kane was beginning to get interested. 'Was that also in Arabic?'

She shook her head. 'No, it was in Greek. An account of a special mission performed by a Greek adventurer called Alexias. He was serving as a centurion in the Tenth Legion of the Roman Army.' She leaned back in the chair. 'Have you ever heard of a Roman general called Aelius Gallus?'

He nodded quickly. 'He tried to conquer Southern Arabia in 24 BC. Got as far south as Sheba and sacked the city of Marib. On the way back he had a rough time. Lost most of his army in the desert.'

She nodded. 'According to Alexias they moved much farther south to Timna and then marched on Shabwa. It was there that Aelius Gallus heard of Sheba's Temple. It was supposed to lie close to the ancient spice route

between Shabwa and Marib, which cuts across a corner
of the desert. There were fantastic tales told of the
wealth of the place. Alexias was commissioned to lead a
small body of cavalry into the desert on a lightning raid.
They were to rejoin the main army at Marib.'

She paused and Kane said, 'Well, go on. Did he find it
or didn't he?'

She smiled. 'Oh, he found it all right. The route
across the desert was marked by seven stone pillars and
the temple was about eighty or ninety miles from
Shabwa. It lay in a gorge in a great outcrop of rock
which, according to Alexias, reared unexpectedly out of
the sand dunes. When they arrived, the temple was
deserted except for one old priestess who tended the
flame on the high altar. The scouting party who were
first into the place were so disappointed at not finding
the treasure, they tortured the old woman to make her
talk. Alexias arrived too late to prevent it. She died
cursing them.'

In the silence which followed, Kane was conscious of
a sudden irrational shiver. He said, 'Did they manage to
find the temple treasury?'

She shook her head. 'It was too well hidden. They
spent two days searching for it without success and then
started back to Shabwa. The first night out they were
caught in the open by a terrible sandstorm. It raged for
more than a day. They lost some of the horses and had

to double up. When they reached the first well, they found it had been poisoned.' She raised her shoulders slightly and shrugged. 'Cutting out the messy details, only Alexias came out of the desert alive and walking on his own two feet.'

'He must have been quite a man,' Kane said.

She nodded. 'I'll let you have the translation of his manuscript to read. You can judge for yourself. He doesn't explain how he rejoined the army, but he obviously managed it successfully. He ended up as commander of the fort at Beer-sheba in Palestine, writing an account of his adventures.'

Kane got to his feet and walked across to the edge of the parapet. He looked out across the harbour to the Gulf of Aden beyond, shrouded in its perpetual heat haze.

The Catalina swung in across the town and splashed into the waters of the harbour. Beyond it a freighter moved slowly across the horizon towards the Indian Ocean, and three dhows, in formation, swooped in towards the harbour like great birds.

He saw none of these things. Before him stretched the Empty Quarter – and somewhere in its fastness was Sheba's Temple.

When he lit a cigarette, his hands were trembling and his body was seized by a strange excitement. It was a feeling he had experienced only twice before in his life.

In both instances he had been a member of an expedition on the brink of an important discovery.

But this – this was different. It was something momentous – the find of a lifetime. Something to rival Knossos or the discovery of Tutankhamen's tomb in the Valley of Kings.

When he turned to face her he was surprised at the steadiness of his voice. 'Have you any idea of the importance of all this if what you tell me is true?'

She frowned. 'I suppose you mean the treasure?'

'To hell with the treasure!' He came back to the table and dropped into his seat. 'All we know about the Queen of Sheba is contained in the Bible. There hasn't been a single inscription found referring to her by name, not even in Marib, which is supposed by most experts to have been her capital. Such a discovery would create a world sensation, and not only in academic circles.'

'I see,' she said slowly. 'That explains why my husband kept his discovery to himself.'

Kane snorted. 'The damned fool. Only a properly equipped expedition can handle this sort of thing successfully.'

'But don't you see?' she said. 'He was trying to prove something to *me*. This had to be his own discovery, alone and unaided. If fame came to him, then he had achieved it by his own efforts, owing help to no man.'

Kane laughed harshly. 'If he tried to penetrate the

Empty Quarter on his own, then he was a fool. If he hasn't died of thirst, he's probably lying face-down in the sand somewhere with his throat cut.'

Deep pain appeared in her eyes and she nervously clasped and unclasped her hands. 'You said Shabwa was a bad-security area, Captain Kane. What exactly did you mean by that?'

He shrugged. 'The borders of the Aden Protectorate and Oman are in dispute with Saudi Arabia. There's been constant tribal friction for years. Military security in the area is handled by the British, and believe me, they've had their hands full. Because they can't be everywhere at once, they've labelled certain places bad-security areas. In other words they can't be responsible for what happens to anyone stupid enough to go there.'

When she looked across at him her face was troubled. 'And Shabwa is one of these areas?'

Kane nodded. 'Very much so. People do visit the area, of course. At the moment there's an American geologist called Jordan up there looking for oil. He's managed to survive by tossing Maria Theresa silver dollars around like confetti and surrounding himself with a picked band of cut-throats, who make sure he stays alive because it's to their own advantage.'

'Have you ever been there?'

He nodded. 'Often, but then I'm pretty well known amongst the tribes in that area. They're mostly Musabein, and friendly enough if they take to you. The trouble is that the fringes of the Empty Quarter are inhabited by outlaws. Men cast out by their tribes for various reasons – mostly unpleasant. If *they* get hold of you, they'll skin you alive and peg you out in the sun. Nice people.'

There was complete horror on her face. 'And you think something like that must have happened to my husband?'

He shrugged. 'There's a fair-to-even chance.' She shuddered violently and buried her face in her hands. Kane got to his feet and stood beside her, a hand on her shoulder. 'Believe me, Mrs Cunningham, I'm only trying to be honest with you. Anything could have happened to him.'

She pushed herself to her feet and stared up into his face, one hand clutching his arm. 'But he could be alive? It is possible, isn't it?'

For a moment he was going to tell her just how slim that chance was and then he smiled and patted her reassuringly. 'Sure, it's possible.'

She started to cry. Kane slipped an arm around her shoulder and led her gently into the bar. 'I think it would be a good idea if you went to your room and rested for a while. I'll make a few enquiries. I might be able to find something out. If your husband was in Dahrein two months ago, someone must have seen him.'

She nodded slightly as they went out into the hall and

mounted the stairs to the first floor. When they reached the door of her room, she took a key from her purse and fumbled at the lock. Kane took it gently from her, opened the door and followed her inside.

There were several suitcases standing in one corner of the bare room and she went across and opened the top one. After a moment's search she came back, a bulky envelope in one hand. 'This is the translation of the manuscript,' she said. 'I think you'll find it rather interesting.'

He slipped it into his pocket and smiled. 'I'll see you this evening around seven for a drink. I may have some news for you.'

She smiled. 'I'll be waiting. I think I'll try and get some sleep in the meantime.'

For a moment he matched her smile with his own and then he gently closed the door.

SIX

HE MOVED ALONG the corridor and as he reached the head of the stairs a door clicked open behind him. A voice said, 'So you and Mrs Cunningham got together sooner than you had intended?'

Skiros was standing in the doorway of his private room, a cheroot clamped firmly between his teeth, a faint smile on his face.

Kane nodded slowly. 'I thought I'd better find out what she was after.'

The Greek removed his cheroot and groaned. 'Mother of Christ, but it's hot. How about joining me in a drink?'

For a moment Kane was about to refuse and then he changed his mind. Very little happened in Dahrein that Skiros didn't know about. He nodded and moved forward. 'Come to think of it I could use one, if you make it long and cool.'

Skiros turned back into the room, wiping his face

with his handkerchief. He sagged down into a large wicker chair by the window and gestured towards a table on which stood several bottles and a pitcher of ice-water. 'You mix the drinks, my friend,' he said. 'I haven't enough energy to lift the bottle.'

Kane closed the door and went over to the table. He quickly mixed two large gin-slings and handed one to the Greek. Skiros swallowed half of it and grunted. 'Christ, that was good. At the beginning of each year I tell myself it will be my last in this accursed hole. I swear on the grave of my mother that I will go home to Greece, but ...' He sighed deeply and shrugged his shoulders.

'Why don't you?' Kane said.

Skiros grinned, exposing a row of decaying teeth. 'Because I am greedy. Because I can make so much money so very easily here.' He sipped some more of his drink and went on. 'But I might ask you the same thing. What can be the attraction of a place like Dahrein for a man like you?' He grinned and his eyes sparkled. 'Could it be the admirable Mademoiselle Perret?'

Kane shrugged calmly. 'Women mean nothing to me, Skiros. I'm in Dahrein for the same reason you are. I can make money here – very easily and tax-free. There aren't many places left where one can do that these days.'

Skiros chuckled. 'And avoid Europe, the war.'

'You think it will come?' Kane asked.

'Of course. Everything Hitler wanted he's got. Why should Poland be different?'

'Not my affair,' Kane said.

'Nor mine.' Skiros drained his glass. 'And what of the beautiful Mrs Cunningham? It isn't every day we get so charming a visitor in Dahrein.'

Kane helped himself to a cigarette from an ivory box on the table. 'Didn't she tell you why she's here?'

Skiros shook his head. 'She came straight to the hotel from the boat. After she'd booked in she asked for you at once. She didn't give a reason. I assumed at first that you must be old friends. To be frank, I thought that perhaps your past was catching up on you.'

Kane walked across to the window. He stood looking out over the harbour and spoke without turning round. 'She's looking for her husband. Apparently he ran out on her. The last she heard, he was making for here.'

Skiros grunted in surprise. 'But why would he come here?'

Kane turned to face him and shrugged. 'He's a lecturer in archaeology at one of the English universities. Apparently he wanted to visit the ruins at Shabwa.'

Skiros frowned. 'But only that crazy American, Jordan, manages to survive up there.'

Kane nodded. 'That's true, but what about Professor

Muller? He's been hunting for rock inscriptions in that area for months now. He's managed to survive somehow.'

Skiros snorted. 'Bah, the German swine.' He spat on the floor and then rubbed it into the carpet with the toe of one shoe. 'He is protected by the Devil, but one day he will go too far. One day they will find him with a bullet in the head.'

Kane shrugged. 'Is he in town at the moment?'

Skiros nodded. 'Yes, he came in last night by road. He drove past the hotel about eleven o'clock just as I was having someone kicked out.'

Kane went to the table and helped himself to another drink. 'You don't know anything about this guy Cunningham, then?'

Skiros shrugged his great shoulders. 'I'm afraid not. When was he supposed to arrive here?' When Kane told him he frowned for a moment and then shook his head. 'No, I can't remember him.'

Kane swallowed his drink and walked to the door. 'I think I'll go and see Muller. He might have run across him.'

He opened the door and Skiros said, 'But why should you go to all this trouble, my friend? I confess I am puzzled.'

Kane turned and grinned. He held up one hand and rubbed his thumb across his fingers in the universal gesture that is readily understood in every corner of the world. 'For money,' he said. 'What else?'

When he emerged from the hotel into the street it was still quiet and deserted, but the sun enveloped him in an invisible cloak that caused the sweat to spring from every pore, soaking through his shirt and pants. He walked slowly along the shady side of the street towards Muller's house, frowning slightly as he considered his conversation with Skiros.

If Cunningham had landed in Dahrein, it was strange Skiros didn't know of it. It was a small town and not much escaped him. But perhaps Cunningham had never reached Dahrein? Perhaps he'd changed his mind? After all, there was only the letter to his wife to go on. On the other hand that theory didn't hold water. He'd left Aden on the mail boat – the British Consul had confirmed that. He must have landed in Dahrein. Perhaps he'd already made arrangements to go up-country and hadn't bothered booking in at the hotel. From what his wife had said, he couldn't have had a great deal of money.

Muller's house was in a narrow alley on the north side of the harbour. The entrance was set in a high wall and Kane pulled on an ancient bell chain several times. As he waited for a response he thought about the German. Muller had arrived in Dahrein the first time about a year previously. A stiff, perfectly mannered Prussian, he was interested in graffiti – the ancient rock inscriptions which were to be found throughout the mountains. He constantly made long expeditions by truck, penetrating deep into some of the wildest country on the border. He seldom took more than two or three Arabs with him and carried no weapons. He was considered by the Musabein to be mad, and this probably accounted for his continued existence. No true believer would dare eternal hell, by laying hands on one of the afflicted of Allah.

The door opened and an Arab servant in clean white robes stood to one side, bowing deeply as Kane entered. He moved into a pleasant courtyard in the centre of which a fountain sparkled in the sun. Above his head, a balcony jutted out from one of the first-floor windows and Muller appeared and looked down at him. A pleased smile appeared on his face and he waved cheerfully. 'Ah, Kane, my good friend. The very man. Come up – come up at once!'

Kane followed the servant inside the house. He led the way upstairs to a narrow corridor, opened a door and stood to one side, motioning Kane through.

Muller was standing beside a large table in his shirt sleeves. When he bowed he almost clicked his heels. He smiled. 'I have something that will interest you. I've taken a latex squeeze of an inscription I found in a gorge near Shabwa. Give me your opinion on it.'

Kane examined the long strip of rubber. The professor was using a new method of copying his inscriptions: a latex solution brushed on to the rock, hardened quickly in the sun and peeled away in a long strip carrying with it a perfect copy.

Kane examined the inscription with interest. After a moment he looked up. 'Quatabanian, isn't it?'

The German nodded. 'Yes, I found it on a rock face not far from an ancient camel trail. I haven't had time to translate it properly, but it seems to refer to a war with the Kingdom of Sheba sometime during the seventh century BC.'

Kane sat on the edge of the table. 'You know that's the third time you've been in the Shabwa area, to my knowledge, during the past four months. Don't you think you're asking for trouble?'

Muller snorted. 'I have no interest in who runs the country so long as I am left alone. The tribesmen know it and don't bother me.'

Kane shrugged. 'Don't say I didn't warn you. Tell me, have you run across any Europeans in the Shabwa area during the past couple of months?'

Muller looked at him in surprise. 'Only Jordan, that crazy fellow-countryman of yours. Why do you ask?'

'There's a woman in town looking for her husband,' Kane told him. 'An archaeologist called Cunningham. He's supposed to have gone up-country to Shabwa about two months ago. No one's heard of him since.'

The German threw back his head and laughed harshly.

'Nor are they likely to, if he went alone. But what did he want at Shabwa?'

Kane shrugged. 'I understand he was looking for graffiti, like you.'

'I can do without the competition, thank you.' Muller got to his feet and walked across to the window, a frown on his face. 'No, I'm afraid I haven't come across this man.' He shook his head. 'It's rather strange. I'm sure I would have heard if there was another European in the mountains.'

Kane nodded. 'Yes, that's what I can't understand. Even Skiros hasn't heard of him, and that's saying something.'

Muller shrugged. 'I'm sorry I can't help you.'

'That's all right,' Kane said. 'I'm beginning to think the guy never arrived here in the first place.'

The German nodded. 'It certainly looks like it.'

Kane went back downstairs, and the servant appeared at once from the cool darkness of a rear corridor and escorted him to the door. When it had closed behind him, he stood for a moment in the hot street, thinking about his next move. There was really only one thing left to do for the moment. He could check with Captain González. He would certainly remember if a European named Cunningham had landed from the mail boat during the past two months.

He walked back through the town the way he had

come, passed the hotel and continued along the waterfront towards the north jetty. The Spaniard's house was
next to it and looked down over the beach. Kane
knocked at the door and it was opened almost immediately by a heavily veiled woman.

She showed him into a cool, inner courtyard, where
he found González stretched comfortably on a divan, a
can of beer in one hand, the contents of which he was
pouring into a tall glass.

He looked up and said cheerfully, 'See, you have
caught me in the act. Already I am becoming a slave to
your American habits. Will you join me?'

Kane shook his head. 'Not this time if you don't
mind.'

He sat on the end of the divan, pushing his cap to
the back of his head, and González said, 'It is not often
you honour my humble house with a visit, Captain
Kane. Presumably you are in need of my assistance.'

Kane grinned. 'As a matter of fact I am.'

An expression of complacency appeared on the Spaniard's face and he leaned back against the cushions with a
sigh. 'Ah, sooner or later everyone comes to me. I trust
you will not accuse me of pride if I tell you that few
things happen in Dahrein that I do not get to know
about sooner or later.'

Kane nodded. 'I know and that's why I'm here.
There's a woman in town – a Mrs Cunningham.'

González nodded. 'This is so. She got off the mail boat from Aden today.'

'She's looking for her husband. He wrote to her two months ago telling her he was coming to Dahrein. He intended to go up-country to Shabwa. She hasn't heard from him since.'

The Spaniard frowned. 'What was this man's name – Cunningham, you say?' He shook his head slowly. 'I'm afraid she must have made a mistake. No one by that name has landed in Dahrein.'

'Are you absolutely sure about that?' Kane demanded.

González shrugged. 'How could I be mistaken? Do I not meet every boat?'

For a moment Kane was going to argue, but he decided it wasn't worth it. That the Spaniard didn't check half the boats he should was common knowledge in Dahrein. Getting him to admit that fact was something else entirely. He pulled his cap down over his eyes and sighed. 'Thanks anyway. It looks as if Mrs Cunningham made a mistake.'

González nodded wisely. 'It is a thing women commonly do.'

Kane stood outside the house, as the door closed behind him, and looked out across the harbour to the launch. He could see Piroo squatting against the stern rail and knew that the Hindu would be watching him.

He felt tired – really tired. He slipped a hand into his

hip pocket and pulled out the envelope Ruth Cunningham had given to him. He looked at it thoughtfully and
came to a sudden decision. There was only one other
person in Dahrein who might have some information
about the elusive John Cunningham. That was Marie
Perret. He had to see her anyway, but his visit could
wait until the evening when it was cooler.

He walked along to the end of the jetty and Piroo
tumbled over the stern into the dinghy and sculled it
towards him. Kane dropped down into the little boat
and the Hindu started to pull back towards the launch.
'Any visitors while I've been away?'

Piroo shook his head. 'All is quiet, Sahib. It is too hot
for any but a fool to be abroad.'

Kane grinned and the little Hindu's face clouded with
dismay. 'I am sorry, Sahib,' he said. 'I have a foolish
tongue.'

Kane shook his head and pulled himself up over the
rail of the launch. 'No, I think you've hit the nail on the
head this time, Piroo. I'm dead tired. I'm going below
for a sleep. Wake me around eight, will you?'

Piroo nodded and Kane went below into the coolness
of his cabin. He mixed a drink, stripped the clothes from
his body and went and lay on the bunk, the envelope
Ruth Cunningham had given him in his hand.

He took out the typed translation of the manuscript
and started to read. It was an absorbing story, and he

read steadily for an hour until he had finished it. For a little while he lay staring at the roof of the cabin and thinking about Alexias. A well-defined personality had emerged from the pages to stand before him. It was that of a brave and aggressive, physically tough man, highly intelligent and a natural leader.

There had been a touch of the dreamer in him also. Kane reread the portion of the manuscript in which Alexias described his feelings on first setting out into the desert in search of the temple. The man's character emerged strongly in the light of his own words. A born adventurer, always restless, always gazing beyond the next hill, always searching for something and never finding it.

Had he been looking for Sheba's Temple or had he really been searching for something else. His own true self, perhaps? The self that most men went through life without ever meeting. He turned to the last page of the manuscript and read again the final sentence.

'. . . So, I, Alexias, Senior Centurion of the Tenth Legion, Commander at Beer-Sheba, end this account. Lest other men should be tempted to follow the seven pillars to Sheba's Temple, a word of warning. For my poor comrades those seven pillars led only to death.'

Kane stared up at the roof, watching the dust dancing in the sunshine that streamed through the porthole above his head, and thought about the Greek's words. There was an Ethiopian proverb that said something about the road to hell being marked by seven pillars, and the Ethiopians had conquered Southern Arabia for a while. For a brief moment, he wondered whether there could possibly be a connection, but dismissed the notion as improbable. The Ethiopian conquest had come much later. He was still thinking about it as he drifted into sleep.

He came awake suddenly and lay staring into the darkness. Some special sense, deep in his subconscious, had sounded an alarm and he lay on the bunk, fingers curled tightly, wary as any animal that knows the hunter is near.

He became aware of the smell first — stale and faintly rancid. Olive oil or perhaps a grease of some sort. And then he heard the breathing and there was a faint curse as someone stumbled against the table. He waited, hardly daring to breathe, and stared up through half-closed eyelids at the bright beam of moonlight which streamed in through the porthole.

And then the breathing was very close and he saw the upraised knife gleam in the moonlight. He twisted and lifted his knee sideways. It connected with his assailant's stomach and there was a subdued grunt. His right hand fastened about the man's wrist and he twisted sharply. There was a cry and the knife fell to the floor.

Kane scrambled from the bunk, hands reaching for his assassin's body, but the man's torso was slippery with oil and Kane's hands failed to secure a grip. The man twisted like an eel and dashed for the entrance. As he came out on deck, Piroo jumped to bar his way. There was a grunt of pain from the little Hindu as their bodies collided, and the killer ducked under his arm and dived over the rail.

Kane stood listening intently, but could hear no sound. He turned slowly. 'Are you all right?'

The little Hindu was almost weeping. 'Sahib, I am shamed. This man boarded the launch and almost killed you while I slept.'

Kane patted him on the shoulder. 'Don't be damned silly. He was probably a professional. They're the only ones who oil their bodies before going on a job. Don't worry about it. Get the dinghy ready and we'll pay a call on our friend Selim.'

He went below and dressed quickly, and when he came back on deck, he was carrying the Colt automatic in his jacket pocket. It was time someone cut Selim down to size, he decided, as they crossed the harbour and rowed between the fishing boats towards the *Farah*.

The dinghy bumped against the side of the great dhow and he told Piroo to wait, mounted a rope ladder quickly, and climbed over the rail. The deck was deserted. Underneath the stern–deck, a door opened into the captain's cabin and he approached cautiously. For a moment he hesitated outside, listening, and then he kicked open the door and went in, the Colt ready in his right hand.

Two Arabs were sitting cross-legged on cushions beside a low table which contained a coffee-pot and several tiny cups. They glanced up in alarm and he held the gun steady on them.

'Where is Selim?' he demanded in Arabic.

One of them shrugged. 'He left this afternoon. I think he went up-country to visit friends.'

For a moment Kane gazed at them suspiciously. As he lowered the Colt and started to move away, he became aware of a familiar odour. It was the stale, rancid smell of olive oil.

He turned slowly and faced the men. 'Take off your robes!' They looked at each other in alarm and the one who had spoken, started to protest. Kane moved forward quickly, a savage look on his face. 'Do as I say.'

The one who had done the talking shrugged and started to remove his outer garments, but the other suddenly made a break for the door. Kane stretched out a foot and tripped him, and as the man scrambled to his feet, hit him across the face with the barrel of the Colt. The heavy foresight slashed open the man's cheek and he slid to the deck, moaning.

Kane slipped the Colt into his pocket and walked to

the door. He turned and said calmly to the other man, 'Tell Selim he'll get out of Dahrein if he knows what's good for him.'

He closed the door behind him, crossed the deck and dropped down into the dinghy. 'Is everything settled, Sahib?' Piroo said.

Kane nodded. 'I think you might say that. You can take me to the jetty now. I'm going into town.'

He stood on the jetty and listened to the sound of the dinghy disappearing into the darkness as the Hindu rowed away and then he turned and walked along the waterfront to the hotel and his appointment with Ruth Cunningham.

SEVEN

THE HOTEL WAS ABLAZE with lights, and the foyer was crowded with people. Kane pushed his way through to the entrance of the casino. Skiros was sitting at a table by the window. His eyes, moving rapidly from table to table, gleamed with satisfaction as the dealers raked the chips across the green baize covers. When he saw Kane, a smile appeared on his face and he waved. Kane nodded briefly and turned away.

The bar was doing a brisk trade and Romero, Noval and Conde, the Catalina crew, were sitting there in flying jackets. Romero waved and Kane joined them.

'Run any good cargos lately?' Romero asked.

'The pot calling the kettle black,' Kane said. 'Guptas told me he saw you and some Portuguese freighter offloading thirty miles out.'

Romero smiled. 'We all need to make a living, amigo.'

'Take care,' Kane said. 'If he saw you, so could someone else.'

He walked away. Noval said. 'He's right.'

Romero shrugged. 'No problem. A few more days and it will all be over. Let's have another drink.'

The corridor was quiet, and the noise from below sounded curiously muted and unreal as if it came from another world. A light showed through the transom window above her door and he knocked softly and waited. It was opened almost immediately and she looked out.

She was wearing a brocaded house-coat in heavy silk, tied with a crimson sash at the waist. Her hair hung loosely to her shoulders, and her face was pale and drawn as if she had slept badly. She smiled and stood to one side and he went in.

She closed the door and leaned against it, her eyes gazing into his searchingly. After a few moments she sighed. 'You haven't got any news for me, have you?'

For a fraction of a second he hesitated and then he shrugged, 'I'm afraid not.'

She moved across to a wicker chair by the window and there was an edge of desperation in her face. 'Surely you've managed to find out something? This is a small town. Somebody must have known him.'

Kane shrugged. 'That's the peculiar thing about the whole business. Nobody seems to have heard of your husband. I finally had a talk with the Customs Chief here. He swears your husband hasn't disembarked in Dahrein during the past two months.'

'But that's impossible,' she said. 'We know he has.'

Kane shook his head. 'We know he intended to come here. We know he got on the boat at Aden. He may have gone on to another port – Mukalla, for instance.'

'Do you think that's possible?'

He shrugged. 'Anything's possible. On the other hand I'm still not convinced your husband didn't land in Dahrein. Captain González is inclined to skimp his duties. If he meets half the boats that come in here he's doing well, but he won't admit it.'

She looked up at him eagerly, 'Then you think my husband may have landed here after all?'

Kane nodded. 'If he landed and went straight up-country the same day, it would explain why no one has heard of him.'

An expression of relief appeared in her eyes and she relaxed against the cushions. 'I'm sure that's what must have happened.' She smiled wanly. 'What's the next move?'

He went across to the window and looked down into the crowded street. 'There's one more person left to see,' he said. 'Marie Perret.'

Ruth Cunningham looked up at him in surprise. 'A woman? But how can she help?'

Kane smiled. 'No ordinary woman, I can assure you.

Marie Perret is half-French, half-Arab. She's the head of a trading organization which stretches from Zanzibar to Singapore. A very remarkable woman. She has regular trucks going up to the Shabwa area. If your husband wanted to get there in a hurry, that's the way he would go.'

There was a strange smile on her face when she looked up at him. 'Is she a friend of yours?'

Kane shrugged. 'I know her,' he said. 'She'll give me any information she has.' He walked to the door. 'If it's not too late when I get back, I'll drop in again.'

She stood up quickly and moved across to the table. 'I've written a letter to the Consul in Aden telling him I've found you all right.' She laughed rather self-consciously. 'He asked me to do so. He didn't seem too happy about my coming here on my own.'

He slipped the letter into his pocket and grinned. 'Maybe he had a point. I'll see you later.'

He went downstairs, crossed the foyer and entered the casino. Skiros was still sitting by the window, cheroot between his teeth and glass at his elbow.

Kane slipped into the opposite chair. 'Looks like you're having a good night.'

Skiros smiled. 'I do not complain. Luckily the world is full of fools who do not understand that the house always wins. What of Mrs Cunningham's husband? Have you managed to trace him yet?'

Kane shook his head. 'González says he hasn't landed here, but you know how much one can rely on his word. I'm going to see Marie Perret now. She might know something.'

As he got to his feet, he took Ruth Cunningham's letter from his pocket and pushed it across the table. 'Put that in the mail bag for me. It's important.'

Skiros nodded and snapped his fingers at a waiter. 'You're just in time. I'm sending a boy down to the jetty now. The mail boat sails on the ten-o'clock tide.' He gave the letter to the waiter with a brief command. 'Have you time for a drink?'

Kane shook his head. 'Another time, Skiros. I'll probably be back later on to see Mrs Cunningham again.'

Skiros smiled and the flesh creased around his eyes. 'I trust you will remember that this is business. She's a very attractive woman.'

Kane didn't to bother reply. He turned and forced his way through the crowd, crossed the foyer and went out into the cool night.

As he walked along the centre of the narrow street, he thought about the Greek's last remark. It would be foolish to deny that Ruth Cunningham was an attractive woman and yet, since that brief feeling of excitement and unease when they had first met on the jetty, he had been conscious of no physical feelings about her.

She was the first woman of his own kind he had met for years and yet she left him completely unmoved. But then, women were something he was extremely careful about. After all, Lillian had seemed a very pleasant girl during those first few months before they got married. Remembering what had come after, the thought that she was no longer a part of his life filled him with a conscious pleasure and he paused on a street corner to light a cigarette.

It was the best part of the day. The Hour of the Dove, they called it. The lights of the ships in the harbour were mirrored in the water, and from a nearby café came the sounds of music and laughter as someone celebrated a wedding.

Arabs in colourful robes crowded sidewalk tables, sipping coffee from delicate cups, talking endlessly amongst themselves. With the advent of night, the street had become a bazaar with stalls that sold everything from hand-made brassware to cooked food.

There was an air of excitement, of vitality in the air, and the night, like smooth velvet, brushed his face as he pressed through the crowd.

Gradually, the streets emptied as he moved away from the centre and climbed steadily through narrow, cobbled alleys towards the promontory which curved out towards the sea.

Marie Perret's house was perched on the extreme end

of the finger of rock, looking out over the harbour. It was a two-storeyed building with a flat roof, standing in an acre of garden surrounded by a high wall.

Kane paused outside a solid, iron-bound door and pulled the bell chain. After a while there was a movement on the other side and the door swung open noiselessly.

The man who stood revealed presented an extra-ordinary figure. A full-blooded Somali, his ebony face was topped by a flowing mane of black hair. He stood six foot six and was broad in proportion: a giant of a man in white robes.

His mouth twisted in a grin and he moved to one side, motioning Kane to enter. Kane smiled and said in Arabic, 'Is your mistress at home, Jamal?'

The Somali turned from the door and nodded. He had been branded in the centre of the forehead as was customary with slaves in certain parts of the Yemen. He had tried to escape from his master, and on being caught, had had his tongue cut out in the market place as a warning to others.

His second attempt at escape had been more successful. Dying from thirst in the desert, he had been found by Marie Perret, who had nursed him back to health. He had been her shadow ever since.

He led the way along a flagged path between the fig trees to a covered terrace, motioned Kane to a chair and disappeared inside the house.

Kane inhaled the freshness of the garden. It was a riot of colour and the night air was heavy with the scent of flowers. Several palms lifted their heads above the wall and gently nodded in the cool breeze, leaves etched against the night sky, and a fountain splashed into a fish pool amongst the trees. There was a light step behind him and he turned quickly and rose to his feet as Marie Perret walked out onto the terrace.

She was a small, graceful girl of twenty-five and the soft contours of her body were accentuated by the jodhpurs and khaki bush-shirt she was wearing. Her hair was black, an inheritance from her Arab mother, as were the wide, almond-shaped eyes and rather full mouth.

The rest of her was pure French, and she smiled gaily and flung herself down into a chair. 'How are you, Gavin? What a wonderful night. I've just been for a ride.'

Kane grinned and offered her a cigarette. When he had given her a light, she leaned back in her chair. 'Did everything go all right in Mukalla?'

He took a letter from his inside pocket and handed it across. 'Sorry, I was forgetting. I saw your agent there yesterday. He gave me that for you.'

As she read it, he watched her covertly, marvelling at the change of expression on her face, cold, businesslike and purposeful. Since the death of her father when she was only twenty, she had ruled Perret and Company with a rod of iron. From the Red Sea to the Pacific her name was a legend. Scrupulously honest, but shrewder than any bazaar trader.

She frowned slightly and called, 'Ahmed – here a moment!'

A heavily built, grey-haired Arab came out onto the terrace. He wore European clothes and held a pen in one hand as though disturbed from some important work. He was the general manager of the firm and an old and trusted friend of her father's.

He smiled and nodded to Kane, and Marie handed him the letter. 'Read that, will you? Gavin has brought it from Mukalla. Laval says he can take all the sesame oil he can get. If we move fast we can buy up all available stocks.'

Ahmed nodded and was about to go back inside when Kane said, 'Just a moment, Ahmed. Perhaps you can help me.'

Ahmed turned with a smile and said in perfect English, 'What is it, Gavin?'

'There's a Mrs Cunningham in town at the moment. She's looking for her husband. When she last heard of him he was supposed to be coming to Dahrein, but no one seems to know anything about him.'

Ahmed frowned for a moment and then nodded. 'Cunningham – John Cunningham. Yes, I remember him. He wanted to go up-country to Shabwa.'

'When was this?' Kane demanded.

The Arab shrugged. 'About two months ago.' He turned to Marie and explained. 'It was when you were in Bombay. This Englishman landed from the boat and visited me at the office. He wanted to go to Shabwa. I warned him of the dangers but he wouldn't listen. We had a convoy of four trucks taking equipment to Jordan. I let him go with them.'

'And when did he return?' Marie said.

Ahmed shrugged. 'I'm afraid I have no knowledge on that point. As far as I remember he paid to be taken to Bir el Madani – the nearest Arab village to Shabwa. What happened to him after that I do not know.'

He turned to Kane. 'I'm sorry I can't be more helpful, Gavin.'

Kane shook his head. 'You've been a lot of help. At least I know this guy got as far as Bir el Madani. Before that I couldn't even prove he'd landed in Dahrein.'

Ahmed smiled. 'Well, if you'll excuse me. I've got a lot of work on my hands.'

After he had gone back into the house, Marie said, 'What on earth could this man Cunningham be doing in the Shabwa area?'

Kane shrugged. 'He was an archaeologist. Probably looking for rock carvings.'

'On his own?' she said incredulously. 'Surely not. Only a fool would attempt to travel in that area alone.'

'Or a man who was looking for something really important,' Kane said.

As soon as the words were out of his mouth he regretted them, but it was too late. She leaned across, a slight frown on her face and said, 'You're holding something back, aren't you? Hadn't you better tell me what it's all about?'

He sighed and got to his feet. 'I suppose I had. For one thing, you might be able to help. For another, now that you've scented a mystery, you won't rest content until you've wormed it out of me.'

She stood up with a soft laugh. 'Dear Gavin, you know me so well by now. Let's walk in the garden and you can unburden yourself.'

They went down the steps and walked through the trees, her hand resting lightly on his arm, and he inhaled her sweetness and was aware of feelings he had not experienced for a long time.

He began to talk, starting with the arrival of Ruth Cunningham and ending with an account of Alexias and his journey into the desert.

When he finished, they were sitting on a seat by the fountain and there was silence for a while. Somewhere a bird called through the night and Marie sighed. 'It's certainly a fantastic story.'

'Don't you believe it?' Kane said.

She shrugged. 'The important thing is that Cunningham did. What do you intend to do now?'

Kane shrugged. 'I'll go up to Shabwa. Question the headman at Bir el Madani and find out what happened to Cunningham.'

Marie stood up and they started to walk back towards the house. 'Personally, I don't think you or anyone else will ever see John Cunningham again.'

Kane nodded. 'You're probably right, but his wife won't rest content until she knows for sure.'

Marie leaned against the balustrade of the terrace. 'I agree with you. However, I think I can help to get this thing cleared up quickly. I'm flying to Bir el Madani in the morning to see Jordan about some equipment he needs. He's boring a test hole about fifteen miles from there. He's had his men lay out a rough airstrip for me. I'm only taking Jamal. There's room for you and Mrs Cunningham if you want to come along.'

Kane felt suddenly elated. 'That would be excellent.'

'Jordan will be waiting to take me to his camp by truck. I expect to be there all morning. You can borrow the plane. Three hours should give you ample time in which to make a quick survey of the area.'

'It would certainly save Mrs Cunningham a rough trip by truck,' Kane said. 'I was worried about that. I don't think she's up to it.'

'Is she pretty?' Marie said.

He shrugged. 'Skiros certainly thinks she is.'

'But you are more interested in her money?'

'The fee she's offering me to find her husband is certainly attractive, but I'm intrigued by the story about that temple.'

Marie laughed lightly. 'The eternal seeker. Will you ever be content with what is on this side of the hill, Gavin?'

'Probably not,' he said. 'I suppose that's the main reason archaeology interested me so much when I was a kid. That's why I stay on here, when each year I swear I'll leave. There's so much to do – as long as one has the money, of course, which means working for Skiros occasionally. But beggars can't be choosers.' He grinned. 'If it comes to that, why do you stay? You could make your headquarters in a more congenial spot. Bombay, for instance.'

She shrugged. 'This is an ancient land and my mother was of an ancient people. It's in my blood, I suppose.'

He dropped his hands on to her shoulders and smiled. 'You're a wonderful girl.'

He was suddenly conscious of the warmth of her body through the thin material of her shirt. For several moments they remained like that, staring into each other's eyes and then the smile slowly faded from her face. Kane pulled her towards him and she made no attempt to resist.

His mouth fastened on hers and she melted into him, alive and warm. After a while he pushed her away from him, holding her at arm's length. 'Damn you!' he said softly.

She smiled faintly, sensing the turmoil in his mind. 'My poor Gavin, have I disturbed the ordered pattern of your existence? But women are the devil, you should know that by now.'

'I'm only too well aware of that fact,' he assured her.

'Would you like a drink?'

He struggled with temptation and won. 'I don't think it would be advisable.'

She took his arm and they went down the steps and through the garden to the gate. She opened it and smiled up at him. 'Seven o'clock at the airfield and don't be late. I want to get an early start.'

Standing there in the moonlight she looked utterly and completely desirable. He sighed and said, 'Look, I'm sorry for what happened.'

She reached up quite suddenly and kissed him on the mouth. 'But I'm not,' she said, and pushed him through the door.

For a little while he stood there in the darkness, his hand raised to the bell chain, and then he turned away and walked down through the darkness towards the town.

When he reached the hotel, he went up to Ruth Cunningham's room and knocked on the door. There was no reply. After trying again, he opened the door and went inside, but the room was empty.

He went back downstairs and into the bar. Skiros was sitting by the window, a drink in front of him, gazing pensively out into the night. Kane crossed the room and stood over him.

The Greek looked up and smiled. 'Did you have any luck?'

Kane nodded. 'I've managed to trace him as far as Bir el Madani. He went up with one of Marie Perret's convoys.'

Skiros raised his eyebrows in surprise. 'So, he actually *did* land in Dahrein. I must say I'm surprised. What do you intend to do next?'

'We're flying up with Marie in the morning,' Kane said. 'I've been up to Mrs Cunningham's room to tell her, but she isn't there.'

Skiros nodded into the darkness. 'She passed this way only a few minutes ago. I think you'll find her on the beach.'

Kane thanked him and went on to the terrace. It was cool and the slight breeze carried the faintest trace of salt spray with it. He went down the steps to the sand and walked towards the white line of surf, his eyes searching the moonlit beach.

He paused, slightly at a loss, and her voice came clearly from his left. 'Over here.'

She was leaning against a fishing boat. As he approached she said, 'Have you any news for me?'

He lit a cigarette, the match cupped between his hands against the wind, and nodded. 'Yes, I think everything's going to be all right now. I've traced your husband as far as a small Arab village about ten miles from Shabwa. We're flying up there with Marie Perret in the morning. I should be able to learn something more definite from the headman.'

She gave a sigh of relief, and leaned against him, a hand on his arm. 'My God, that's marvellous.'

She sank down into the soft sand and Kane sat beside her and gave her a cigarette. The match flared in his hands, illuminating the strong line of her jaw, and tears glistened in her eyes.

He took her hand and said gently, 'Look, everything's going to be fine.'

She took a deep breath as if trying to get control of herself and nodded. 'I don't know how I'm ever going to be able to repay you for what you've already accomplished.'

'You'll have no difficulty, I assure you.' He grinned wryly and got to his feet. 'And now I think you'd better get some sleep, Mrs Cunningham. We've got an early start.'

She didn't argue and he saw her to the terrace of the hotel. He made arrangements to pick her up at six-thirty and then walked along the water's edge to the jetty.

Piroo was squatting on a stone, head nodding. He came awake quickly and smiled a welcome, teeth gleaming in the darkness.

As they rowed across to the launch, Kane told him about his trip to Bir el Madani on the following day. 'You'll be in complete charge,' he said as he clambered over the rail and stood on the deck of the launch. 'Keep a sharp look-out for trouble. Particularly from Selim.'

He left Piroo on deck securing the dinghy and went down to his cabin. It was dark and quiet and the moonlight crept in through the porthole and touched him with ghostly fingers.

He lay down on the bunk and stared up at the cabin roof and thought about Marie. For a moment the darkness was touched by her presence and she seemed to smile at him as he drifted into sleep.

EIGHT

THE FISHING BOATS were slipping out through the harbour entrance towards the Gulf as Kane turned off the jetty and moved along the waterfront. He lit a cigarette, the first of the day, and coughed as the smoke caught at the back of his throat. He felt tired and there was a slight ache behind his right eye. For a moment he paused, watching the fishing boats dip into the Gulf current, white sails shining in the early morning sun, and then he continued towards the hotel.

He was wearing khaki pants and shirt and a battered felt bush hat. On impulse, he had slipped the Colt into his hip pocket before leaving the launch. He had many friends amongst the tribesmen of the Shabwa area, but one could never be too sure.

Ruth Cunningham was standing on the steps of the hotel when he arrived. She was wearing a white blouse, open at the neck, and cream whipcord slacks. Her hair was bound with the same blue scarf she had worn on that first occasion, and when she smiled she looked extremely attractive.

'Will I do?' she demanded, spreading her arms slightly.

Kane nodded. 'Decorative, but serviceable.' He glanced at his watch. 'We'll have to step on it. I don't want to keep Marie waiting.'

They didn't speak much as they walked through a maze of narrow alleys and emerged on the edge of town. She had dark smudges under her eyes as if she had not slept well, and there was a strained, anxious look to her that he didn't like.

The airstrip was a quarter of a mile outside Dahrein in the opening of a narrow pass which cut deeply into the mountains. It was not an official stopping place for any of the major airlines and had been constructed as an emergency strip by the Spanish Air Force.

There was one hangar, a crumbling, decrepit building in concrete with a roof of corrugated iron. They could see the plane squatting on the runway from a long way off, a de Havilland Rapide painted scarlet and silver. Its twin engines were already ticking over as they approached.

Jamal was sitting in one of the rear seats and Marie jumped down to the ground and came to meet them. Kane made the introduction and the two women shook hands.

'It's very kind of you to help in this way,' Ruth Cunningham said.

Marie shrugged. 'It's nothing, Mrs Cunningham. Nothing at all. I'm going up to Bir el Madani on business, anyway.' She turned to Kane, a slight smile on her face and her eyes sparkled. 'I hope you slept well, Gavin. Sorry to rush you, but I promised Jordan I'd be there by seven-thirty.'

Ruth Cunningham climbed into the seat next to Jamal, who stared stolidly ahead and ignored her. Marie slipped into the pilot's seat and then turned enquiringly to Kane. 'Would you like to fly her?'

He nodded and she stepped into the passenger area, making room for him. He taxied slowly along the ground and turned into the wind. A moment later and the end of the airstrip was rushing to meet them. He pulled the column back slowly and the Rapide lifted into the pass, rock walls flashing by on either side.

The air was bumpy as they flew out of the pass, for a forty-knot wind was blowing across the mountains. They climbed through heat haze that already blurred the horizon, and levelled off at six thousand feet to cross the coastal range.

Beyond the mountains the sky was a brilliant sapphire and, within half an hour, the real desert appeared in the distance, its colours varying between burnished gold and deep red.

Suddenly, they were passing over a tall oil derrick surrounded by a group of tents and several vehicles, and then Ruth Cunningham cried excitedly, 'Look, there's a truck down there!'

Kane glanced out of the window and saw a truck moving at high speed in the direction in which they were flying. A little later, a dark splotch appeared in the distance. Within a few minutes it had increased into a clump of green palm trees and a scattered group of flat-roofed houses.

The airstrip was a narrow slot between two dunes, with a windsock on a tall pole at one end. Kane circled once and then turned into the wind for a perfect landing between two rows of empty oil drums. As he taxied to the far end of the airstrip, the truck appeared from among the houses and moved towards them in a cloud of dust.

Kane switched off the engines, opened the door and jumped to the ground. He turned and handed the two women down in turn as the truck braked to a halt a few feet away and a man slid from behind the wheel and came to meet them.

He was young, with a bronzed, reckless face, and his fair hair was closely cropped. He was dressed in sun-bleached khaki and a revolver was slung low on his right hip in a black leather holster.

His teeth flashed in a ready smile and he cried, 'The Devil himself. What brings you up here?'

Kane grinned and punched him on the shoulder. 'I was hoping you might be able to help us, Jordan.' He half-turned and indicated Ruth Cunningham. 'Mrs Cunningham here, is looking for her husband. We know he arrived in Bir el Madani two months ago. He intended to visit Shabwa for a few days. She hasn't heard from him since.'

Jordan took her hand, his face serious. 'I'm sorry to hear that, Mrs Cunningham.' He frowned slightly for a moment or two and then shook his head. 'No, I can't say I've heard of your husband. The headman of the village might be able to help.'

She turned to Kane and he nodded. 'I know the headman here – Omar bin Naser. If he knows anything he'll tell us.'

Jordan led her towards the Ford pick-up truck and handed her in. 'That's settled then. I'll drop you and Mrs Cunningham in the village, Kane. We'll see you sometime this afternoon. Marie and I have a hell of a lot to discuss.'

Marie squeezed into the front seat beside Ruth Cunningham, and Kane and Jamal sat in the back under the canvas awning. As they moved away, Kane glanced casually over his shoulder and saw an Arab in faded russet robes and red head-cloth, appear from behind a dune and urge his camel across the airstrip. He slid to the ground and stood by the plane.

Kane tapped Jordan on the shoulder. 'Pull up a minute, will you?'

Jordan halted the truck and they all turned and looked back. The Arab was examining the plane closely and then he looked up and gazed towards them.

Kane scrambled out of the truck. 'I'll see what he wants. It may be just idle curiosity, but you never can tell with Bedouins.'

As he approached the plane, the Arab advanced to meet him, hand resting lightly on the silver hilt of his curved *jambiya*. Kane halted a few feet away from him and said in Arabic, 'What are you doing here? Are you looking for someone?'

The Arab's face was lined and drawn. The pupils of his eyes were like pinpricks and his lips were flecked with foam. 'I have a letter for one named Kane,' he said in a dead voice.

Kane's hand slid round to the butt of the Colt as he spoke. 'I am he. Where is the letter?'

The Arab pulled the *jambiya* from its sheath and the blade flashed in the hot sunlight. Kane took a quick step back and tried to draw the Colt. The foresight snagged on the lining of his hip pocket and he cursed and ducked under the swinging blade, reaching for the Arab's throat.

For a moment they swayed, locked together, Kane

trying to twist the weapon from the man's grasp, and then the Arab lifted his knee viciously.

Kane hung on grimly and they fell to the ground, rolling over and over. He could hardly breathe and yet everything assumed a sharper definition and he was acutely aware of the stink of the man's unwashed body, of the madness in the staring eyes.

In the distance, a woman screamed and he was conscious of something digging painfully into his right buttock. It was the Colt and he wrenched it free from his pocket, rammed the barrel into the Arab's stomach and pulled the trigger twice as the *jambiya* was raised to strike.

The force of the bullets, fired at such short range, lifted the man backwards. Kane tried to get up, but there was a roaring in his ears. Someone cried his name. He grabbed for the plane's wing, hauling himself erect, and another Arab came into his range of vision, running towards him, *jambiya* raised above his head.

Kane tried to lift the Colt, but his arm seemed to have lost its strength and then Jordan arrived on the scene. The geologist dropped to one knee beside him, rested the barrel of his heavy revolver across his left forearm and fired so fast that four shots sounded like one continuous roll of thunder.

The Arab kept coming right into the line of fire, the bullets thudding solidly into his body and then, when he was almost upon them, he seemed to lurch sideways and fell on to his face.

For several moments there was complete silence and then Kane heard a cry behind him. He turned, still holding onto the wing for support and saw Marie running towards him.

Her face was white and drawn and she clutched his arm. 'Gavin, are you all right?'

He patted her on the hand reassuringly. 'Thanks to Jordan.'

The geologist was bending over the man he had killed and he turned, a puzzled frown on his face. 'How the hell did he keep on coming? I didn't miss once.'

Kane turned the body over with his right foot. The face was contorted in agony, the lips foam-flecked and curled back, exposing stained teeth. 'Haven't you ever come across anyone who looks like this before?'

Jordan shook his head, but Marie moved forward and looked down. 'This man has been drugged with *quat*. He must be a hired assassin.'

Kane nodded. 'That's the way I see it. When I asked the first man what he wanted, he told me he had a letter for a man called Kane.'

'But why the hell should anyone want to kill you?' Jordan said. 'And what *is* this stuff *quat* anyway?'

Kane lit a cigarette. 'It's a narcotic stimulant found in the leaves of a shrub from these parts. When the leaves are chewed, the user feels alert and confident. Used regularly, it gradually has an effect on the physical appearance.'

Jordan frowned. 'What's this bit about hired assassins?'

Kane shrugged. 'I'd have thought you'd have known about that by now. If you want to kill a man in this country, you don't do it yourself. You hire a professional.'

Jamal had been busy searching the body of the first man Kane had killed. Now he turned and came towards them, a leather bag in one hand, which he handed to his mistress.

Marie looked inside and then held it forward silently so that the others could see its contents. It was stuffed with silver coins.

Jordan whistled and Marie said gravely, 'There must be the equivalent of two or three thousand Maria Theresa dollars here, Gavin. Someone must want you dead very badly.'

Kane nodded soberly. 'Yes, and I think I know who it is. I had a run-in with Selim, yesterday. One of his men had a try last night when I was sleeping.'

Marie frowned. 'But how would he know that you would be at Bir el Madani this morning?'

Kane considered the fact and then nodded. 'You've got a point there. Anyway, to hell with it. It didn't come off and somebody's paid a lot of money out for nothing.' He groaned and wiped a hand across his mouth. 'I could use a drink.'

'I've got a flask in the truck,' Jordan told him. 'Come to think of it, I could do with a swallow myself.' He grinned and shook his head. 'And I was worried in case being a geologist turned out to be boring.'

As they walked back towards the truck, an excited crowd of people swarmed past them and moved towards the dead bodies.

'Where the hell did they spring from?' Jordan said. 'Anyone would think they knew something was going to happen.'

'They very probably did,' Kane told him.

Ruth Cunningham looked sick and her face was pale. 'Are you all right?' she said to Kane.

He nodded. 'I'm sorry you had to see that.'

She seemed to find difficulty in speaking and clambered back into the front seat, where she sat, nervously clasping and unclasping her hands.

Jordan had been examining the bag of coins Jamal had found on the body of the first assassin and he looked at Kane enquiringly. 'What happens to this little lot?'

'You hang on to it for now,' Kane told him. 'I'm sure we'll find a use for it later.'

Jordan grinned. 'Pretty good pay under the circumstances.' He produced a brandy flask from a compartment under the dashboard, took a long swallow and handed it to Kane. 'Compliments of the house.'

Kane raised the flask and toasted him silently. He choked as the brandy burned its way down into his stomach, and he climbed into the rear of the truck. 'I haven't thanked you yet. That was nice shooting back there.'

Jordan slipped behind the wheel and drove towards the village. 'I was raised on a ranch in Wyoming.'

He turned the truck into the wide main street and braked to a halt outside the largest house, scattering a herd of goats.

Kane got down and Ruth Cunningham followed him. 'After we've had our talk with Omar, we'll take a flight over the Shabwa area,' he said to Marie.

She nodded. 'Take care, Gavin, and don't go too far out into the desert. It's bad flying country.' She glanced at her watch. 'Let's see – with any luck, we should be back here just after noon.'

Kane smiled. 'We'll be back by then easily.'

There was a grinding of gears and the truck shot away in a cloud of dust. Kane turned to speak to Ruth Cunningham and found the headman of the village standing outside his door, waiting to welcome them.

'You honour my poor house, Captain Kane,' he said in Arabic.

Kane smiled. 'Always I come when I need something,

my friend, but let us go inside. The sun is hot and the events of the past half-hour have given me a great desire to sit down.'

Omar led the way into his windowless, mud-brick home. The house was divided into two rooms. In one were kept the goats and chickens belonging to the family, and the other was the general living room. At night Omar and his family simply lay down in their robes on rush mats and slept.

Despite the obvious poverty of the place, Omar bin Naser had the native courtesy and instinctive dignity of the Arab. He motioned Kane and Ruth Cunningham to two cushions and clapped his hands. Within a few moments, a woman entered the room, wearing a long black outer robe which also closely veiled her face. She carried a brass pot in her left hand and three cups in the other.

After the customary feigned refusals that courtesy demanded, Kane accepted a cup and nodded slightly to Ruth Cunningham who followed suit. The woman poured a few drops into their cup and waited for approval. It was Yemeni *mocha* – the finest coffee in the world. Kane smiled and held out his cup, which the woman promptly filled.

Omar waved her away and Kane offered him a cigarette, which the headman accepted eagerly. When it was drawing to his satisfaction, he sat back with a sigh and said courteously, 'In what way may I help you?'

Kane nodded to Ruth Cunningham. 'I seek this lady's husband,' he said. 'He came here about two months ago. Can you tell us anything about him?'

Omar's eyes sparked with interest, and he inclined his head to Ruth Cunningham with a pleasant smile and said to Kane, 'Presumably the woman does not understand Arabic?' When Kane nodded, he went on, 'A man did come here some two months ago. He arrived with a convoy of trucks one day. They went on to the camp of the American Jordan, but this man stayed in Bir el Madani.'

'Where did he go from here?' Kane said.

Omar shrugged. 'Who knows? He was mad – quite mad. He wanted to journey from Shabwa to Marib by camel. He needed guides.'

'And did you help him?' Kane said.

Omar nodded. 'The camels I could supply, but the guides were another matter. No one ventures into the Empty Quarter, as you know, unless he is a hunted man with a price on his head.'

'Then he went alone?'

The headman shook his head. 'There was a mad Bedouin passing through here at the time – a Rashid. You know what they are like. Anything for adventure. Proud, reckless men. He volunteered to go with the Englishman.'

'And have you heard of them since?' Kane said.

Omar smiled faintly. 'Captain Kane, their bones are bleaching in the sun at this moment. It is the only end for those who are foolish enough to venture into the Empty Quarter.'

For a little while Kane sat there, frowning, and then he got to his feet and gave Ruth Cunningham a hand. 'Have you found anything out?' she demanded anxiously.

He nodded. 'Plenty. Your husband was here. He managed to get camels and a Bedouin of the Rashid tribe to accompany him. He told Omar he intended to cross the Empty Quarter from Shabwa to Marib.'

Her eyes were troubled, and Kane patted her reassuringly on the arm and turned to Omar. 'Many thanks, my friend, but we must go now. I shall fly this lady to Shabwa and then a little way out into the desert. Perhaps we shall discover something.'

Omar nodded and accompanied them to the door. As they emerged into the street, several villagers passed, dragging a crude cart on which lay the two assassins.

Their robes were dabbled with blood and clouds of flies hovered over them. Ruth Cunningham shuddered violently and Omar said, 'I rejoice at your narrow escape, Captain Kane.'

Kane turned quickly, a look that was almost amusement in his eyes. 'You knew they were waiting for me?'

Omar nodded. 'But of course,' he said gently.

'And knowing, you made no attempt to prevent it?'

Omar looked pained. 'I could not possibly interfere with another man's blood feud.'

Kane started to laugh. An expression of complete bewilderment appeared on Omar's face, and Kane took Ruth Cunningham's arm and led her away, still laughing.

'What was all that about?' she said. 'I find all this Arabic frustrating.'

'You wouldn't understand,' he told her. 'A private joke.'

As they walked towards the airstrip she said, 'That was wonderful coffee we had. Who was the woman – his wife?'

Kane shook his head. 'A household slave.'

'Surely you're joking,' she said.

He smiled gently. 'Didn't you notice the mark of the hot iron on Jamal's forehead? He was a slave in the Yemen. They cut out his tongue the first time he tried to escape. There are thousands of slaves in most parts of Arabia still.'

She shuddered and they continued the rest of the way in silence. When they reached the plane, the only signs of the fight were several patches of blood in the sand of the runway. Kane pushed her into the cabin and clambered up behind. He wasted no time, and a few moments later they were climbing steeply into the blue sky.

They reached Shabwa within ten or fifteen minutes and Ruth Cunningham looked down with an expression of disappointment on her face. 'I can't say I find it particularly thrilling.'

Kane nodded. 'Not very imposing, I agree, but under the sands down there are the sixty temples the Roman historian Pliny wrote about. A treasure trove for some future expedition.'

He checked the compass and turned the nose of the Rapide out into the desert. 'I've set course for Marib. According to Alexias, the temple should be somewhere out here on a direct line from Shabwa. About ninety miles, he said. Let's hope we come across something.'

He took the plane down to a height of five or six hundred feet above the sand dunes, hoping for tracks or some other sign that human beings had passed this way, but there was nothing. The desert stretched as far as the eye could see, sterile, savage and unbelievably lonely.

After some fifteen minutes, Ruth Cunningham gave him a sudden nudge. In front of them an immense sand dune that must have been seven or eight hundred feet in height, lifted into the sky, and Kane pulled back the column slightly. The engines spluttered and missed a couple of times.

He pulled the column back hard and the Rapide lifted over the top of the sand dune with only a few feet to spare, and then the engines coughed and died.

The utter silence which followed was broken only by the sough of the wind in the struts and then, as the plane dipped sickeningly, Ruth Cunningham screamed.

Kane fought for control. About fifty or sixty feet above the sand, he managed to level out and then another great sand dune was rushing towards them. 'Hang on!' he said tightly, and pulled on the column with all his strength.

The Rapide swerved violently. For a moment it seemed to right itself, and then the left wingtips dipped to the sand. The aircraft spun in a circle and there was a tearing crunch of metal. Kane cried a warning and braced himself to withstand the impact as they ploughed to a halt through the soft sand.

NINE

KANE GAVE A LONG, shuddering sigh and wiped sweat from his eyes with the back of one hand. He turned and looked into the white, strained face of Ruth Cunningham. 'Are you all right?'

She nodded briefly. 'I held on tight as we went in.'

He opened the door and jumped to the ground. The nose of the Rapide was half-buried in soft sand and the left wing was crumpled and useless.

'I can't understand why we didn't catch fire,' he said with a frown and came back to the door and looked at the instrument panel. 'That's funny, the fuel tanks are empty.'

She moved across the cabin and clambered out through the door. 'What's that supposed to mean?'

'I don't really know. When the engines failed it could have been lack of fuel, but I don't see why. I wonder what state the radio's in.'

As he climbed back into the cabin to examine it, Ruth

Cunningham said, 'Is there anyone near enough to pick up the signal?'

He nodded. 'Jordan has a short-wave receiver at his camp.' He examined the set briefly and turned with a grimace. 'I'm afraid we've had it. They weren't built to stand up to this kind of treatment.'

Ruth Cunningham ran a hand over her face wearily. 'I'd give anything for a drink of water.'

'We can soon fix that,' he said, reaching behind the back seats for a large jerrycan and plastic cup. 'This thing's full, so water is the least of our problems.'

He gave her a long drink and had one himself. Afterwards, they sat in the shade of the wing, smoking cigarettes and not talking.

After a while, she turned and looked at him and said in a level voice, 'Gavin, give it to me straight. What are our chances?'

'A lot better than you think. I reckon we're about thirty miles from Shabwa. It's no good trying to make it during the heat of the day. The best thing we can do is rest up here and make a move at dusk. We'll be able to travel a lot faster at night because of the coolness.'

'Do you think they'll come looking for us?'

He nodded confidently. 'Of course they will. As soon as Marie and Jordan return to Bir el Madani and find we're missing, they'll form a search party. Those Ford trucks of his are specially fitted for desert work.'

She looked into his eyes searchingly and then she smiled. 'I'm glad I'm with you, Gavin. With anyone else, I think I would have been scared – really scared.'

He smiled and helped her to her feet. 'But there isn't anything to be scared about. A few hours' discomfort, that's all. It's the sort of thing you'll be able to talk about for years, and the details will grow with the telling.'

'I suppose you're right.' Her shoulders sagged and she looked tired.

He pushed her towards the cabin door. 'Try to sleep for a few hours. You'll find it cooler in there. I'll wake you later on this afternoon.'

He closed the door behind her, lay down in the shade of the right wing and pillowed his head on his hands.

He wished he felt as confident as he had tried to sound. On his own and with plenty of water, he would have stood a fair chance of reaching Shabwa in a forced march during the night, but with a woman . . . !

One thing was certain. Marie and Jordan would come looking for them, but the trick lay in knowing where to look and the desert was a big place.

He listened to the stillness and felt the heat press down on him with a force that was almost physical, and after a while drifted into a troubled sleep.

Somewhere, there was a scream of terror, and something

hard poked him under the chin. He opened his eyes and looked along the barrel of a rifle.

The man on the other end was a Yemeni in coloured turban, his half-naked body smeared with indigo dye. At some time in the past, his ears had been cropped – the sign of a thief – and his right cheek branded.

Two others were dragging Ruth Cunningham from the cabin, and as Kane scrambled to his feet, her shirt ripped and she fell to the ground. One of the men laughed and dragged her upright by the hair.

The man's face had been eaten away by yaws, his eyes burned out of a mass of putrefying flesh and there were two holes where his nose had once been. Ruth Cunningham stared with horror into that ghastly face and fainted.

Kane took a step towards her and the three Yemenis all swung their rifles ominously. 'It would be unwise to move,' the one with the cropped ears said in harsh, guttural Arabic.

Kane moistened dry lips. 'Take us to Bir el Madani and there will be a rich reward for you.'

The one with the face out of a nightmare uttered an oath and spat. He took a quick step forward, reversing his rifle, and rammed the butt into Kane's stomach. One of them took the Colt automatic from his hip pocket. Then they left him for a while, his face in the sand, breathing deeply and waiting for the agony to pass.

The three men were outlaws – so much was obvious. But how were they going to act, that was the important thing? They seemed to be having an argument and Kane opened his eyes, his breathing easier, and tried to listen.

Dirty brown feet encased in leather sandals appeared before his face and a hand pulled him into a sitting position. He found himself facing the man with the cropped ears.

He squatted in front of Kane, rifle cocked in his arms and grinned. 'It is time for us to go now.'

'Take us to Bir el Madani,' Kane urged desperately. 'You will receive a large reward, I promise you. Five thousand Maria Theresa dollars.'

The Yemeni shook his head. 'Over the border I am a dead man walking.' He nodded towards Ruth Cunningham. 'We can make as much money selling the woman in the slave market at Sana.'

'Ten thousand,' Kane said. 'Name your price. She is a very rich woman in her own country.'

The Arab shook his head. 'How can I be sure she would honour the bargain? A white woman commands a high price in the Yemen.'

'And what about me?' Kane said.

The Yemeni shrugged. 'My friends wished to cut your throat, but I have persuaded them otherwise. Whether you live or die is your own affair. Shabwa is but a short step for a strong man.'

Kane frowned. 'I don't understand.'

The Yemeni grinned. 'You do not remember me? Two years ago when the Bal Harith were camped near Shabwa? There was some question of a stolen horse. If they had caught me, it would have meant my life. You allowed me to hide in your truck until darkness. The ways of Allah are strange.'

Kane remembered the incident at once. He leaned forward, lowering his voice. 'Help us to safety and I'll see you are richly rewarded. At least you owe me that.'

The Yemeni shook his head and stood up. 'A life for a life. Now I owe you nothing. Rest content. My friends wished to relieve you of your manhood, at least. If you are wise, you will stay quiet until we have gone.'

He joined his two companions who had already mounted their camels, one of them slinging Ruth Cunningham's unconscious body across his wooden saddle. Kane stood by helplessly as they rode away from the plane and disappeared into a fold of the dunes.

He glanced at his watch. It was just after noon, which meant that he had slept for longer than he had supposed. For a moment he stood there, considering and rejecting possible courses of action. But there was really no solution – just the slightest chance that he might be able to do something with the radio. He climbed into the cabin and set to work.

From the beginning it was hopeless and yet he kept on working, long after it became obvious that the set was damaged beyond repair, hoping to nurse into life a spark which would live long enough to carry a message to the outside world.

Sweat dripped from his body and the heat in the cabin enveloped him so that he had to stop on several occasions for rest and water. It was shortly after three when he finally admitted defeat. He sat back wearily and started to light a cigarette. At that moment, he heard the sound of an engine approaching through the stillness.

He jumped down to the ground and stood there listening, a sudden wild hope inside him. It was close, very close. As he shaded his eyes with one hand and looked up, a truck topped a dune a hundred yards away and came towards him.

Marie was driving, with Jamal sitting beside her. As Kane went towards them, she cut the engine, slid from behind the wheel, and ran to meet him. 'Are you all right, Gavin?' she demanded anxiously.

He nodded. 'I'm fine, but I don't understand. How did you get here so quickly?'

'It's a long story,' she said. 'Is Mrs Cunningham in the plane?'

He shook his head. 'I'm afraid not.'

He quickly described what had happened, and when

he had finished, Marie looked grave. 'If we don't catch them before darkness, there's no knowing what they might do to her.'

He nodded. 'If we get moving straight away, we should find them without much difficulty.'

He sat beside Marie in the front seat, Jamal climbed into the back, and within a few moments they were moving, following the clearly defined tracks of the three camels.

The truck was fitted with twelve forward gears and this, coupled with four-wheel drive, made it ideal for crossing the shifting sand dunes.

Kane leaned back in his seat. 'You'd better fill me in on what happened at Bir el Madani.'

'I finished my business with Jordan by eleven,' Marie told him. 'He sent Jamal and me back to the village in this truck with one of his drivers. When we reached the airstrip, Omar was waiting for us. He said there was a stranger in the village – a coast Arab who had been heard to boast that you would not be returning.'

'And Omar actually volunteered this information?' Kane said.

She smiled faintly. 'You'll never understand the complexity of the Arab mind, Gavin. To kill your enemy face-to-face is one thing, but a trick such as tampering with the plane,' – she shrugged – 'to Omar, such a thing would lack honour.'

'I'll go along with that,' Kane said, 'but how did you find out for certain what had happened?'

'Omar pointed out the man in question, and Jamal took him behind a hut and questioned him. He was stubborn, but with his right arm broken and the threat of similar treatment to his left, he saw reason.'

Kane glanced sharply at her in amazement. 'My God, you don't believe in half-measures, do you?'

'My mother was a Rashid,' she said calmly. 'We are a hard people, especially when the things we value are threatened.'

To that, there could be no reply, and Kane said, 'He'd tampered with the fuel tank, I suppose?'

'He took advantage of the confusion when the villagers were swarming around the bodies of the assassins. No one noticed him in the crowd.'

'Did you manage to find out who'd paid him?'

She nodded. 'Just as you thought – Selim.'

Kane frowned. 'He must really hate me to go to all this trouble. How did you manage to find the plane so easily?'

'I knew you were flying on a direct line from Shabwa to Marib. I took a bearing, followed the compass and hoped for the best. I sent Jordan's driver back to the camp with a note explaining what had happened.'

Kane grinned wryly. 'You're fast becoming indispensable.'

For once she could find nothing to say and concentrated on her driving, following the twisting tracks with ease until they finally came to a broad plain of flat sand mixed with gravel, which stretched away into the distance. She moved into top gear and pressed her foot flat against the boards.

The truck raced across the flat plain in a cloud of dust, and soon the three of them were coated with sand from head to foot. Kane helped himself to water and his eyes ceaselessly searched the plain ahead, looking for the black dots in the distance which would indicate their quarry.

There were two rifles bracketed to the roof of the truck and he took them down and handed one to Jamal. The great Somali's hands checked the weapon expertly and then he cradled it in his arms, one finger inside the trigger guard.

Kane gripped his tightly and stared through the windscreen out of dust-rimmed eyes. His mind became a blank as he waited so that he was taken completely by surprise when Marie screamed in his ear, and the black dots in the distance seemed to rush towards them.

He raised his rifle slightly and waited. As they came up fast behind the three camels, the man at the rear turned and looked towards them and his mouth opened in a cry of dismay. He urged his camel forward.

Marie spun the wheel and the truck moved abreast of

the Arabs. Kane raised his rifle and fired a warning shot over them, and then the truck had drawn ahead.

As Marie swerved to a halt, the man with the diseased face, who was carrying Ruth Cunningham in front of him, released her so that she tumbled to the ground. He raised his rifle in one hand, and Jamal fired a quick shot, which lifted him from the saddle.

Marie drove the truck forward and halted beside Ruth Cunningham. She was weeping, her head buried in her hands, and Marie spoke gently to her. 'Did they harm you in any way?'

Ruth Cunningham shook her head several times and spoke with difficulty. 'The man with the awful face kept pawing me, but the one who seemed to be the leader made him leave me alone.' She collapsed in a flood of tears and Marie led her gently to the truck and eased her into one of the seats.

Kane walked across to the two men, who sat their camels quietly under the threat of Jamal's carbine. The man with the cropped ears grinned down at him. 'The ways of Allah are strange.'

'You're damned right, they are,' Kane told him. 'It's lucky for you, you didn't harm her. Now get to hell out of here.'

He stood for a little while, watching them ride away, and then he went to help Jamal who was digging a shallow grave for the dead man.

When they returned to the truck, Ruth Cunningham was still sobbing quietly on Marie's shoulder. Kane raised his eyebrows enquiringly and Marie shook her head. He shrugged. 'There's no hurry. We'll rest up for an hour before starting back.'

He sat down in the sand, his back against the side of the truck and pulled the brim of his bush hat over his eyes, and gradually, his head nodded forward and he dozed.

In what seemed to be the same moment of time, he came awake to a gentle tug at his shoulder. Marie smiled down at him. 'We should be making a move, Gavin. It's after six.'

He got to his feet and looked into the interior of the truck. Ruth Cunningham was curled up in one of the passenger seats, sleeping. He smiled at Marie and climbed behind the wheel. She and Jamal went round to the other side and Kane gently eased in the clutch and drove away.

There was a car compass fitted to the dashboard and he decided to leave the camel tracks and pursue what seemed to be a much more direct route to Shabwa.

Gradually the sun dipped towards the horizon in a great orange ball and then the night fell with its usual rapidity. The sky was clear, with stars strung away to the horizon like diamond chips, and the moon bathed the desert in an unearthly white light.

Marie had dozed off, her head against Kane's shoulder, and he leaned back in his seat, hands steady on the wheel, and stared ahead into the night.

When he saw it, the shock was so great that he slammed his foot against the brake, bringing the truck to a halt with such force that everyone was thrown forward in their seats and brought violently awake.

'Gavin, what is it?' Marie cried in alarm.

He pointed over to the right-hand side of the vehicle without speaking. Standing poised on top of a small rise, throwing a long, dark, moon-shadow across the sand, was a delicate stone pillar.

Kane got out of the truck, followed by Marie, and walked slowly towards it. When he was a few feet away, his foot kicked against something with a metallic clang.

He picked up a couple of cans and weighed them in each hand. 'Corned beef and soup. Whoever it was, no Arab, that's for sure.'

He leaned down and picked up another object as Ruth Cunningham and Jamal moved forward to join him. For a moment they could not see what it was, and then he turned and held it out towards them. It was a large and very empty aluminium water-bottle.

TEN

JAMAL GENTLY CLEARED loose sand away from the base of the pillar while Kane knelt beside him, directing the beam of a powerful electric torch on the work.

After a while, the Somali stopped digging and pointed. Kane leaned forward and saw that a long inscription in perfectly chiselled characters had emerged. He studied it carefully for several minutes and then got to his feet and walked back to the truck.

A spirit-stove flared in the slight breeze. Marie and Ruth Cunningham were heating cans of beans in a pan of boiling water. Kane flung himself down beside them, and Ruth poured hot coffee into a tin mug and handed it to him. 'Have you found anything more?'

Kane drank some of the coffee and nodded. 'A long Sabean inscription — that was the language of ancient Sheba, by the way. Unfortunately I haven't any books with me and I'm a little rusty.' He held out the mug for more coffee. 'I managed to decipher one or two words.

Asthar, for example, and a reference to distance which I'm not familiar with.'

Marie pushed back her hair with one hand and the light from the spirit-stove, flickering in the wind, danced across her face. 'You mean it's probably a sort of milestone?'

Kane nodded. 'It's obviously one of the seven pillars mentioned by Alexias.'

'But is that possible?' she said. 'If that pillar was erected during the time of the Queen of Sheba it would be almost three thousand years old.'

He shrugged. 'That's perfectly possible in the dry heat of the desert. I've seen inscriptions at Marib over two thousand five hundred years old and they look as fresh as if the mason had chiselled them yesterday – and another thing, you know how frequent sand storms are here. It's probably been buried, then uncovered again, scores of times over the ages.'

'What about that water-bottle and the empty food cans?' Ruth said, handing him a plate of beans.

'I think your husband must have left them there. We know for certain that he left Shabwa by camel. Whatever else may have happened to him, I think it's reasonable to assume he'd have got this far.'

'But those three outlaws?' she said. 'Perhaps there are others like them.'

He nodded. 'That's true. With every man's hand

against them they go where no one else dares, but as a rule they don't come this far out. They usually hug the edge of the desert and keep within striking distance of water. In any case, only a European would use a water-bottle of that type. The Bedouins use goatskins.'

'So it was all true,' Marie said after a short silence. 'Sheba and her temple, Alexias and his Roman cavalrymen.'

'Yes, they must have passed this way,' Kane said.

In the eerie silence that followed his words, no one seemed to breathe and for one timeless moment he almost expected to hear the chink of harness in the distance and see the Roman cavalrymen appear over the dunes, Alexias in the lead, moonlight glinting on his breastplate as he reined in his horse and gazed out over the desert.

And then out of the silence there came a low, vibrant hum, which grew until it filled the ears, and Ruth Cunningham turned in alarm. Marie placed a hand on her arm and said quickly, 'It's nothing to be alarmed about. Something to do with the change in temperature. One layer of sand sliding over the other.'

'The singing sands,' Kane said softly. 'I wonder if Alexias heard them also.'

'One thing *is* certain,' Ruth Cunningham said. 'He wouldn't have had anyone who could have given him the scientific explanation.'

'All the same, I don't think he'd have been afraid,' Kane said gently. There was a short silence and he took out a crumpled packet of cigarettes. 'The thing we've got to decide now is, what do we do next.'

Marie took one of his cigarettes and leaned down to light it from the spirit-stove. When she sat up, her face was thoughtful. 'How far did Alexias say the temple was from Shabwa?'

'About ninety miles,' Kane said.

'And we're about forty miles from Shabwa?' He nodded and she leaned back, her face half in shadow. After a while she said slowly, 'I think we should turn round and chart a course for Marib. Even if we don't find other pillars still standing, we should find this outcrop of rock which Alexias described.'

Ruth Cunningham turned eagerly to Kane. 'Do you think we could?'

He nodded. 'I don't see why not. We've got plenty of fuel and water. If we start now, we should be there by dawn. There's enough moonlight, and it would be a damned sight more pleasant than travelling during the day.'

Marie got to her feet. 'That settles it, then. We pack up and move on right away.' As Kane turned away, she caught his sleeve. 'You need some sleep, Gavin. I'll drive for a couple of hours – you can take over later.'

For a moment, he was going to refuse, and then tiredness dropped about his shoulders like a heavy blanket. When they drove off half an hour later, he was sprawled amongst the baggage in the rear and already asleep.

He awakened with a bad taste in his mouth. It was bitterly cold and he sat up and leaned forward. Jamal dozed beside him and Ruth Cunningham was asleep, her head lolling backwards.

He scrambled over into the front seat. When Marie turned to smile at him, he saw the lines of fatigue on her face and a strange and immediate rush of tenderness moved inside him.

'What time is it?' he said.

'About three-thirty.'

He reached across and took the wheel in his hands. 'Slide out of the way and I'll take over. You should have wakened me an hour ago.'

She lit a cigarette and placed it in his mouth and then she folded her arms and leaned against him, her head on his shoulder. 'All at once I feel tired.'

He inhaled the fragrance of her and smiled. 'Lucky me.'

She sighed contentedly. 'This is nice.'

They were crossing an area of flat scrubland and he drove with one hand, sliding the other about her shoulder, pulling her close. There were many things he could have said, but there was really no need to say anything.

After a while, she raised her face and kissed him gently on one cheek. 'My poor Gavin,' she said and there was a glint of amusement in her eyes.

'Damn you!' he said. 'Damn all women!'

She laughed softly. 'What are we going to do about it?'

He sighed. 'The usual thing, I suppose. There's Father O'Brien at Mukalla. Will he suit you?'

'Admirably – I like Father O'Brien,' she said. 'And afterwards?'

He shrugged. 'That can take care of itself.'

She seemed about to argue the point and then she shrugged as if content for the moment. 'We'll see.'

After a while, she slept and Kane held her close as he stared out through the windscreen, and told himself wryly that life was catching up on him again. It was rather pleasant to find that he didn't really mind.

The scrubland came to an end and he eased Marie into the corner, changed to a lower gear, and took the truck up the steep side of a dune.

The moon grew paler, and in the east, tiny fingers of light appeared above the horizon as dawn touched the sky. His eyes were gritty and sore from lack of sleep and his arms ached with the driving of the past few hours.

He halted on top of a large dune for a moment or

two and searched the desert with field glasses. As the sun lifted above the horizon, flooding the sky with light, it glinted on something in the distance. He focused the glasses. Rearing out of the desert five or six miles away, was a great outcrop of reddish stone.

He engaged a low gear and took the truck down the steep side of the sand dune. Once at the bottom, he drove through a gap which brought him to another flat plain of sand and scrub. He accelerated and drove towards the distant outcrop of rock at high speed.

As the truck lurched forward, the others came awake quickly. 'What's happening?' Marie demanded anxiously.

He nodded into the distance. 'We're almost there.'

Ruth Cunningham leaned forward, her hands gripping the edge of the seat so strongly that her knuckles showed white.

The outcrop increased in size until it towered above them and then they entered the deep gorge which twisted into the heart of it. Kane braked to a halt and switched off the engine. It was completely quiet, and after a moment, he took down one of the rifles and stepped to the ground. 'It might be an idea if we left the truck here. There's no knowing what we might find up ahead.'

Jamal took the other rifle and they started to walk along the firm bed of the gorge. After a while, Ruth

Cunningham gave a startled exclamation and pointed upwards. 'Isn't that an inscription on the face of the rock?'

As the sun's rays penetrated the gorge, they picked out the rock inscriptions with startling suddenness. Kane moved closer and gazed up. After a moment or two, he nodded. 'They're Sabean all right. We've certainly come to the right place.'

He moved on, the others at his shoulder. They passed several more inscriptions and then rounded a shoulder of rock and paused.

Before them stretched a broad avenue of pillars, some in varying stages of ruin, others still intact. At the end of the avenue there was the crumbling façade of a mighty temple built into the face of the gorge itself.

Kane's mouth went dry. He could remember no other moment in his life quite like it. He started forward quickly and the others trailed after him.

At the end of the avenue of pillars, and directly in front of the temple itself, was a deep pool of water, crystal-clear and fed from some invisible spring. He flung himself down by its side and drank from his cupped hands.

He could hear the others coming up behind him, the two women talking excitedly, and he cried out, 'This water is as cold as ice.'

Their voices ceased abruptly and, as Kane started to get up, a reflection in the water in front of him caused him to grab for his rifle.

A bullet chipped the stone edge of the pool, and he raised his arms above his head and climbed slowly to his feet. On the other side of the pool were at least a dozen half-naked Bedouins, and they were holding the very latest Lee Enfield rifles. Standing in front of them, a sardonic smile on his face, was Selim.

'Please do not try anything foolish,' he said in his careful, clipped English.

The Bedouins moved quickly round the pool, splitting into two groups and effectively surrounding Kane and his party. Selim followed at a more leisurely pace, one hand toying with the hilt of his *jambiya*, the other tugging gently at his beard.

He paused a foot or so away and Kane said softly, 'It's a small world.'

Selim nodded. 'You are a hard man to kill.' He sighed heavily and his right fist shot out, catching Kane full in the mouth.

Kane lay on the ground for a moment, shaking his head and conscious of the threatening muzzles of the rifles that had swung towards him. He wiped blood from his mouth and got to his feet slowly.

Selim smiled. 'The down payment on an old score. The rest will come later. I never forget a debt.' He gave a quick command and the Bedouins closed in, urging their prisoners forward with shrill cries.

As he stumbled towards the great flight of steps which led up to the temple, Kane considered the unexpected turn events had taken. From the beginning, he should have realized there was the possibility that John Cunningham had survived the desert crossing – that some human agency had prevented his return. But why Selim? It didn't make sense.

As he mounted the top step and crossed the terrace, the closer view of the temple drove other considerations from his mind. It had been built into the face of the rock wall itself, and the great pillars that supported the portico and flanked the entrance were at least sixty feet high.

Marie appeared at his shoulder and her voice was filled with awe. 'I've never seen anything like it. There's nothing to touch this in the whole of Arabia.'

Kane nodded. 'Strong Egyptian influence, I would say. Same style of portico as the temple at Karnak.'

It was cool and very quiet inside and his eyes soon became accustomed to the dim light. The floor was constructed of rose-coloured marble, and pillars of well-cut blocks of drafted masonry, towered into the gloom. At the other end of the imposing nave, a great statue loomed out of the darkness.

The party paused, as Selim called a halt and ordered most of his men outside except for three who were obviously to be their guards. He turned to Kane. 'You will all stay here. If you attempt to escape, or make a suspicious move of any sort, the guards have orders to kill you at once.'

'Okay, you're the boss,' Kane said. 'There's one thing you might tell us before you go. What happened to Mrs Cunningham's husband? After all, he's the reason we're here.'

Selim shrugged. 'He is alive and well – for the moment.'

Ruth Cunningham moved forward. 'When can I see him? Oh, please let me see him.'

Her cheeks were flushed and her eyes sparkled. Selim looked down into her face as if seeing her for the first time. After a moment or two, he shook his head slowly. 'That is not possible at the moment. If you behave yourself, you may see him later. You must wait here.'

'But for what?' Kane demanded. 'A firing squad, a slit throat or a new arrival?'

Selim smiled thinly. 'I am not here to answer questions.'

He turned and walked away quickly, and Kane took the crumpled pack of cigarettes from his pocket. There was one left and he drew smoke deep into his lungs as he looked up at the statue.

It was like nothing he had ever seen before, carved from solid stone. The lips were full and sensual, and the eyes slanted upwards above high cheekbones and were closed as if in sleep. It had a strong affinity with the statues of the Hindu goddess Kali, which he had seen many times in Indian temples.

He frowned slightly, his mind grappling with the academic side of the problem, and his eyes wandered to the high altar, noticing the carved fire-bowl. He remembered the Roman cavalrymen and the old priestess who had remained to tend the flame, and time seemed to have no meaning. It was a circle, turning upon itself endlessly.

Marie moved beside him and said softly, 'It gives me a strange feeling to know that he must have stood here – Alexias, I mean.'

Kane nodded without speaking and they stayed there for a moment, side by side, thinking the same thoughts, and then there was a sudden commotion in the entrance.

As Kane turned, a man in dust-covered khaki clothes moved towards them. He wore an Arab head-cloth and sand goggles covered his eyes. When he was a few feet away, he paused and regarded them silently for a moment before removing the goggles. It was Professor Muller.

He bowed stiffly. 'I trust you ladies have not been seriously inconvenienced?'

Kane took a quick step forward, but before he could

speak, a familiar voice said, 'Ah my good friend, Captain Kane. So you managed to get here after all?' and Skiros stepped out of the gloom.

ELEVEN

IT WAS ALMOST NOON when the two guards came to the temple for Kane. Marie and Ruth Cunningham had been removed earlier that morning, and shortly afterwards, Jamal had also been taken away.

Alone in the temple with his guards, Kane had spent the time going over events again and again in his mind, but it was no use. He couldn't make sense of any of it. If Muller had stumbled across the temple by chance, then why hadn't he announced his discovery? It would have made him world-famous. And what about Skiros and Selim? Where did they fit in? The problem offered no solution and he waited with mounting impatience until the two Bedouins came for him.

Emerging from the cool half-light of the temple, he paused at the top of the steps, momentarily dazzled by the strong sun. One of his guards pushed him forward so that he stumbled down several steps, almost losing his balance.

The two men seemed to find the incident amusing and Kane, by a supreme effort of will, choked back his anger and walked docilely between them, his eyes keenly searching the valley as they advanced.

The rock walls were covered with inscriptions and at several points he noticed the dark openings of caves. Quite suddenly, the floor of the gorge dipped slightly, and beneath them in a hollow he saw an encampment of several tents beside a green oasis of palm trees.

It was the numbers of men and camels which surprised Kane as he moved down into the camp. On every side, men sweated in the hot sun, loading the great beasts with heavy boxes as if preparing to move out.

He lost count of the tribes represented. Half-naked Yemenis in coloured turbans, their bodies tattooed and smeared with indigo dye, Rashid Bedouins, Musabein, Bal Harith – they were all there. As his guards hustled him through the throng, heads turned curiously.

They halted outside the largest tent and motioned him inside. Kane pulled back the flap and entered. Muller was sitting at a small, folding table, drinking coffee and examining a potsherd with a magnifying glass. He looked up and smiled. 'Ah, Kane, come in! Come in!'

Kane sat down on a camp stool opposite, and Muller lifted the pot and smiled again. 'Coffee?' Kane nodded and the German filled a cup and pushed it across.

Kane leaned forward, arms resting on the table. 'What have you done with the women?'

Muller looked pained. 'We are not barbarians. They are under guard in a nearby tent. They will find it more comfortable than the temple.'

'That's most considerate of you,' Kane said. 'And what have you done with Cunningham?'

'You will be joining him presently,' Muller said calmly. 'But first, Skiros wishes to see you.'

Kane said, 'What the hell is all this about, anyway?'

Muller got to his feet and reached for his hat. 'But that is why I sent for you, my friend. That is what you are about to find out.'

He pushed back the tent flap and Kane followed him. They moved through the oasis, climbing up towards one side of the gorge, the two Bedouins at their heels, and men passed them going down to the oasis, heavy boxes on their shoulders.

They mounted a narrow ramp which seemed to be cut out of solid rock. At the top there was the entrance to a cave with a sentry standing beside it, and men worked stripped to the waist, dragging out more boxes, which they stacked ready to be carried down to the encampment. Muller brushed past them and Kane followed.

The cave was of no great size, but there seemed to be a variety of technical equipment piled on every side.

Skiros was sitting before a complicated short-wave transmitting and receiving set. As they came in, he removed the earphones from his head and swivelled on his stool. 'Ah, Captain Kane. So you have arrived?'

There was a pleasant smile on his face as if this were some kind of party and Kane an eagerly awaited guest.

'Quite a set-up you have here,' Kane said.

Skiros nodded. 'We *are* rather proud of it.' He took a packet from his breast pocket and held it out. 'Cigarette?'

Kane took one and said, 'Don't you think it's time someone told me what this is all about?'

Skiros nodded. 'But of course. Why else are you here?' He gestured towards the stacked boxes. 'Help yourself.'

The boxes were made of metal and painted a dull grey. Kane pulled one forward and unclipped the lid. It was expertly packed with rifles, new and shining with grease from the factory. The next one contained sub-machine guns.

He took one out and examined it closely. It had been manufactured in Germany. He turned, his eyes hard. 'I underestimated you. I thought maybe you were smuggling archaeological finds out of the country illegally, but this . . .'

Skiros smiled complacently. 'Yes, it's quite something,

isn't it? We were extremely lucky finding such a place, thanks to Muller.'

'Until Cunningham arrived. That must have been quite a shock.'

Skiros shook his head. 'A slight inconvenience, that's all.'

Kane turned again to the stacked cases of arms and kicked one of the boxes. 'I suppose this is why the British have been having so much trouble with the tribes on the Oman border?'

Skiros smiled. 'We do our small best, but the arms are simply a payment to the tribesmen for helping us. What they do with them is their own business.

Kane looked at the boxes again. 'Those sub-machine guns are German.'

'MP40s, the best.'

'So you're not even Greek?'

'My mother was and her name was Skiros, but I'm proud to say my father was a German. It doesn't matter what his name was.'

Kane turned and looked at Muller who had been standing silently by his side. 'And how does Muller fit into the picture?'

'Quite neatly,' Skiros said. 'He discovered the existence of this place from an old Bedouin who staggered into his camp near Shabwa one night, dying of thirst.'

Kane said, 'For God's sake, why did you have to deal

with a vulture like this, Muller? Any one of a dozen foundations in Europe or America would have gladly given you financial backing.'

Muller looked embarrassed. 'There were reasons.'

'Indeed there were.' Skiros laughed. 'As you won't be going anywhere I see no reason not to tell you the truth, my friend. Like me, the professor is a German – a good German. We serve the Third Reich and our Führer, Adolf Hitler.'

'My God,' Kane said.

'I work for the Abwehr, you know what that is?'

'German military intelligence.'

'Exactly. We're going to win the coming war, my friend. The day after tomorrow is the 1st of September. That's when we invade Poland.'

'Madness,' Kane said. 'You'll all go down to hell together.'

'I don't think so. You see, we have the big battalions. We also have Captain Carlos Romero and his friends, who are Spanish volunteers in the SS. They will arrive here in the Catalina tomorrow. The following day they will land on the Suez Canal, seed it with mines and blow it up. That should give our English friends in Egypt and London something to chew on.'

Kane struggled to take it all in. 'I can't believe it.'

'A matter of indifference to me.'

Kane took a deep breath. 'What happens now?'

'To you?' Skiros shrugged. 'For a day or two, Muller has a use for you, but after that . . .' His voice trailed away and he sighed as if genuinely sorry.

'That wouldn't be very wise,' Kane said.

Skiros raised his eyebrows slightly. 'Presumably you have a reason for saying that?'

Kane tried to sound completely sure of himself. 'I sent a letter to the American Consul at Aden telling him exactly where we were going.' He shrugged. 'It was a natural precaution – anything can happen in the desert, you know that.'

'You're lying, of course.'

Kane shook his head. 'I gave you the letter to put in the mail bag for me – remember?'

'Very clever, my friend,' Skiros said softly.

Complete panic had appeared on Muller's face and he subsided on to an ammunition box and wiped sweat from his face and neck with a handkerchief. 'We've got to get out of here,' he said and his voice was shaking.

'Pull yourself together.' Skiros selected a cigarette and tapped it on the packet thoughtfully.

Kane smiled. 'If we don't return within a reasonable period of time, the American Consul in Aden will set the usual machinery in motion. They're bound to come looking for us.'

Skiros smiled thinly. 'Quite correct, but as you yourself have so helpfully pointed out, the Consul will make no move until a reasonable period of time has elapsed.'

Kane cursed softly because Skiros was right and he knew it. The troubled frown disappeared from Muller's face and he sagged with relief. 'God in heaven, but you're right.'

Skiros nodded complacently. 'You should know by now that invariably I am. The American Consul will make no move for at least a month. We on the other hand, will be out of here within two days.'

'Two days!' Muller said and he seemed to be genuinely perturbed. 'That doesn't leave me much time. I don't know if we'll be through by then.'

'Frankly, my dear Muller, the question of whether or not you manage to break into your wretched tomb before we leave, doesn't interest me.'

'Can I put Kane to work with the other two?' Muller asked.

Skiros turned to Kane. 'I'm sure you won't object. After all, this sort of work is more in your line.'

Kane tried to think of something to say, but for the moment, he was beaten. 'I guess this is your round.'

Skiros grinned good-humouredly. 'That's it, Kane. Be philosophical about the thing.' All at once, his manner changed and he became brisk and businesslike. 'And now you must excuse me. I have much to do.'

He swung round in his chair and picked up the

earphones. Muller touched Kane on the arm and led the way outside. He turned to the right and walked along a broad ledge to where two armed men squatted before the entrance to another cave. It was no more than four feet high and Kane bent down to peer inside.

Muller wiped sweat from his face with a handkerchief and said awkwardly, 'I'm sorry about this, Kane.'

'I'm not in the mood to take confession today,' Kane told him. 'What am I supposed to do in here?'

Just inside the entrance was a spot-lamp, and the German switched it on and led the way in. The cave was only thirty or forty feet across, and the roof a couple of feet above their heads. The powerful beam moved slowly across the wall, and with startling suddenness, the outlines of two human figures with bows in their hands sprang into life.

Kane went forward and examined the figures with interest. 'Polychrome wall painting,' he said, touching them gently with his fingers. 'Remarkably well preserved.'

'What date would you give them?' Muller asked.

Kane shrugged, his animosity for the moment forgotten. 'It's hard to tell. I've seen the same sort of thing in the Hoggar Mountains in the Sahara, but comparisons are difficult. I'd say at least eight thousand years old. Are there any more?'

The German swung the lamp, picking out several

rock etchings, and the beam came to rest upon a pile of rubble at the rear of the cave beside a narrow opening. 'I think you will find this much more interesting.'

It was obviously the work of man, and blocks of drafted masonry had been removed to open a passage beyond.

'And you think this is the entrance to a tomb?' Kane said.

'What else could it be?' Muller asked. 'The temple is Sabean if not older. If this valley was some sort of holy place, it would be natural to assume that burials took place here.'

Since entering the cave, Kane had been conscious of faint sounds, and now a light appeared in the dark passage and Jamal emerged, a lamp in one hand, dragging a large basket filled with rubble. He stood for a moment and looked at them calmly, his great body streaked with dust and sweat, and then he emptied the basket and disappeared back into the darkness.

'Presumably Cunningham is in there also,' Kane said.

Muller nodded. 'His help, although unwillingly given, has been of great assistance over the past few weeks.'

'There's just one thing I can't understand,' Kane said. 'You've plenty of Bedouins in camp. Why haven't you used a few of them as labourers?'

Muller sighed. 'In the first place, Skiros is not exactly sympathetic to my work and refuses his permission. In any case, they are all incurably superstitious. They believe these caves to be haunted by evil spirits.'

Before Kane could reply, a voice interrupted from behind. 'If you care to examine the roof, you'll find a much more cogent reason for their reluctance to work in here. The whole damned lot is ready to fall as soon as anyone coughs.'

The man who emerged from the passage was of medium height and wiry, stripped to the waist, and like Jamal, coated with dust from head to foot.

Muller ignored the remark. 'How are things progressing today, Cunningham?'

'No better than yesterday or the day before,' Cunningham replied. 'As far as I'm concerned, we're getting nowhere fast. You'll need a squad of labourers and pneumatic drills if you want to get anywhere with this lot.'

'I agree with you, my friend, but what can I do?' Muller said. 'However, I've brought you a new recruit. Kane here has had a great deal of experience at this sort of thing. I'm sure you'll be able to work something out between you.'

'I'd like to point out that I haven't eaten for some considerable time now,' Kane said.

'I'll have some food sent up later this afternoon,' Muller told him. 'In return, I shall naturally expect to see some results.' He went outside, leaving them alone.

Cunningham leaned against the wall and ran a hand wearily over his face. 'And who the hell might you be? Are you anything to do with the big fellow they dumped in here this morning? I haven't been able to get a word out of him.'

'That isn't surprising,' Kane said. 'He hasn't got a tongue, but there's nothing wrong with his hearing as long as you can speak either Somali or Arabic.'

Cunningham laughed. 'Well, my Arabic isn't too bad. I'll have to bow out on the Somali question.'

Kane held out his hand. 'My name is Kane,' he said. 'Your wife hired me to find you when she received the letter you'd left with the British Consul in Aden.'

Cunningham straightened and his voice was strained with excitement. 'Ruth sent you? Have you seen her recently?'

'Only a couple of hours ago,' Kane told him. 'She's up above with a friend of mine called Marie Perret. I'm afraid Muller and Skiros grabbed the lot of us.'

'How is she?' Cunningham demanded. 'Is she all right?'

'She was in good spirits when I last saw her, but very worried about you.'

Cunningham sat down on the pile of rubbish. 'I think you'd better bring me up to date, old man.'

Kane spoke quickly, telling him everything that had happened since his first meeting with Ruth Cunningham on the jetty at Dahrein including what Skiros had just told him.

When he had finished, Cunningham said, 'It's quite a story.'

Kane nodded. 'I suppose it is, but what happened to you?'

Cunningham laughed bitterly. 'I was a damned fool, I can see that now. For various reasons, it was important to me that the discovery of this place should be my own unaided work. When I arrived at Bir el Madani, I realized I couldn't hope to penetrate the desert on my own. I managed to find a Rashid Bedouin brave enough – or stupid enough – to accompany me.'

'Presumably you charted a course across the Empty Quarter from Shabwa to Marib and hoped for the best?'

Cunningham nodded. 'It was surprisingly easy. We had a spare camel and carried plenty of water. On the second day we found that pillar.'

'The one where we discovered the aluminium water-bottle?'

Cunningham nodded. 'We camped there for the night. It was empty and I was cutting down on weight. Frankly, I never expected to find any of the pillars left standing.'

'That was the only one we saw,' Kane told him.

'I did find another one,' Cunningham said. 'It was lying on its side, half-buried.'

'What happened when you got here?'

'It was a bad business. As we entered the gorge, they swarmed all over us. My Rashid was a brave man. He tried to put up a fight, but they shot him down. They put me into cold storage at the bottom of a disused well until Skiros arrived the following day. On two occasions since I've been here, the Catalina you mention has landed on the flat plain outside the gorge. I think Skiros intended to kill me, but then Muller arrived and suggested he might have a use for me on this job. Skiros let him have his way.'

'I'm afraid you've only postponed the evil day,' Kane told him.

Cunningham shrugged wearily. 'I don't give a damn about myself – it's Ruth I'm worried about.'

Kane nodded. 'I know how you feel, but we're not through yet. We'll think of something. Where do they put you at night?'

Cunningham laughed shortly. 'Until a week ago I slept in one of the tents under guard. I tried to make a run for it one night, but I'm afraid I didn't get very far. Since then, I've been back in the well.'

'Sounds lousy,' Kane said.

Cunningham shrugged. 'At least it's dry. I shouldn't imagine there's been any water in the damned thing for a thousand years or more.' He got to his feet and stretched. 'We'd better get started. Muller can be surprisingly nasty if he doesn't think enough work's been done.'

He picked up the spot-lamp and led the way into the passage. It was perhaps sixty or seventy feet long and sloped downwards. At the far end, Jamal was filling a basket, the blade of his shovel flashing in the lamplight. There was barely enough room for two men to work side-by-side. Jamal turned at the sound of the approach, Kane slapped him on the shoulder and the Somali went back to his digging.

'As you can see, conditions aren't too good,' Cunningham said.

Kane examined the walls closely with one of the lamps and frowned. 'I've excavated rock tombs in the mountains around Shabwa, but I've never come across one with an entrance like this.'

Cunningham nodded. 'I think Muller is barking up the wrong tree. He doesn't even know for certain that the temple was constructed by Balquis, Queen of Sheba. I do.'

'That's the one comforting thing I've heard today,' Kane told him. 'But I must say I'd like to know where this damned tunnel leads myself.'

'There's only one way to find out,' Cunningham said, handing him a shovel.

Kane paused only to strip to the waist and then he moved in beside the Somali and started to dig.

★

In Berlin at Turpitz Ufer, Canaris was working at his desk when Ritter came in. 'I've just heard from Skiros,' Ritter said.

The Admiral sat back. 'Everything on schedule?'

'Absolutely.'

'What happens to Romero and his friends after they leave the Catalina?'

'They'll be picked up by a member of our Egyptian bureau and driven straight to Italian territory.'

'Excellent.' Canaris smiled. 'Not long now, Hans.'

'No, Herr Admiral.'

'Carry on,' Canaris said and Ritter went out.

TWELVE

THE MOON HAD RISEN over the rim of the gorge and the valley was filled with its eerie radiance, when Muller had them taken down to the encampment. Emerging from the cave, Kane stretched to ease his tired muscles and paused at the sight of the temple, bathed in moonlight. It looked incredibly beautiful and awe-inspiring, but the guards apparently felt otherwise. The muzzle of a rifle dug painfully into his back and he was urged on down the slope.

It was quiet in the valley and the shadows and loneliness moved in from the desert as they passed between the tents and entered the trees. Somewhere, a camel coughed and an Arab stood knee-deep in the pool and washed himself, pausing to watch curiously as they passed.

On the other side of the trees they halted beside a small horseshoe of rock that surrounded a round, black hole, perhaps five feet in diameter. A heavy rope was secured to a nearby palm tree and one of the guards picked up the free end and tossed it down into the darkness.

Cunningham went down first, straddling the rope, holding it tightly between his hands and walking backwards over the rim of the hole. When the Somali had followed him, Muller turned to Kane and spread his hands in a characteristic gesture. 'I am sorry about this, my friend, but Skiros insists. He considers you to be a very resourceful man.'

'Save your breath,' Kane said coldly. He picked up the rope without another word and began the descent.

The shaft had been hewn roughly from solid rock and his feet gripped the sides easily. He paused once and looked up at the stars gleaming in the round opening and then, all at once, they seemed very far away, and beneath him, there was a slight movement.

Hands reached out for his feet, guiding him down as the shaft widened, and he dropped into soft sand. As he picked himself up, the rope disappeared into the darkness above, brushing against his face. The sensation was so unpleasant that he moved back sharply and bumped into someone.

'Stay where you are,' Cunningham said. 'They usually send down a basket with food in it.' A moment later he grunted in satisfaction. 'Got it!' He took Kane by the elbow. 'Six careful paces and you'll find the wall.'

Kane moved through the darkness, hands outstretched until his fingers brushed on stone. He sat down, back against the wall, aware that Jamal was beside him, and Cunningham shared out the food. When they had finished eating, they discussed the situation.

'Have you ever tried to get out?' Kane said.

Cunningham got to his feet. 'If it were daylight I could show you. The shaft widens about five feet above our heads. If it were not for that, there might be a chance of scaling the main shaft. It's narrow enough and the walls are of roughly hewn stone.'

Kane fumbled in his shirt pocket and took out a book of matches. As the first one flared, he held it high above his head. Cunningham was right. The bottom of the shaft widened considerably. The match burned his fingers and he dropped it with a muffled curse.

He turned to Cunningham 'I suppose you know we're living on borrowed time? We've got one more day at the most. Frankly, we've got two choices. We either get out of this hole or die.'

'I'm with you there,' Cunningham said. 'But how the hell do we manage it?'

Kane moved across to Jamal, squatted in front of him, and started to speak slowly and clearly in Arabic. When he had finished, the big Somali squeezed his shoulder to indicate that he had understood, and got to his feet.

Kane turned to Cunningham. 'Jamal is so incredibly

strong, he might be able to push me high enough into that shaft to get some kind of grip in the narrow part. I'll climb on to his shoulders and I want you to stand behind to steady me.'

'It's worth a try, I suppose,' Cunningham said.

Jamal stood beneath the shaft and Kane scrambled up on to his shoulders. Very carefully he pushed himself erect and raised his hands above his head. They just reached inside the shaft.

'Now!' he said in Arabic and Jamal's great hands moved under his feet, lifting him bodily into the air.

Kane clawed desperately for a grip. Panic moved inside him as the Somali's arms started to tremble and then his hands fastened into a crack in the rock, and he heaved desperately. A moment later, he was securely wedged in the shaft, his back against one side, his feet against the other.

He worked his way steadily upwards, pausing every so often for a rest. The rough stonework dug painfully into his back, but he hung on grimly, and gradually the opening of the shaft increased in size until he was resting a foot or so beneath the rim.

He quickly pulled himself over the edge and crawled towards the rope. At that precise moment, two Bedouins appeared from amongst the palm trees and stood in a patch of moonlight a few feet away from the shaft, talking idly.

He had flattened himself into the sand at the first sound. Now, he carefully inched forward into the shadows and worked his way into the trees. For the moment, there was nothing he could do for Cunningham and Jamal. The two Bedouins were armed and one carried a rifle crooked in his arm. It would be impossible to tackle both of them.

He got to his feet and walked quietly away through the palm trees towards the encampment. As he approached, he could hear singing. The Bedouins were squatting round a great, flaring fire and several of them danced together, weaving an intricate pattern in and out of the firelight. One man played on a herd boy's pipe, another beat monotonously on a small skin drum. The rest sat cross-legged in a circle, clapping their hands in time to the music and swaying their bodies rhythmically.

He skirted the fire, keeping to the shadows, and moved in among the tents. The first two he examined were empty and he by-passed the largest one.

Two guards stood before a tent on the far side of the encampment. He circled round behind and crawled into the shadows at the base of the tent. He could hear movement inside, and then Ruth Cunningham murmured something he couldn't quite catch and Marie replied.

He gently slackened one of the guy ropes and lifted

the bottom edge of the tent a couple of inches. By lying flat on the ground, he could just see inside.

Marie was sitting on a sleeping bag, her back only six inches from him, and Ruth Cunningham was nearer the entrance.

Kane said softly, 'Marie, don't look round. Tell Ruth to keep on talking.'

Marie's shoulders stiffened under the thin material of her shirt and then she leaned forward and spoke softly to the other girl. Ruth Cunningham gave a startled gasp and then she seemed to get control of herself. She started to talk loudly, discussing what had happened and speculating on the future.

Marie stretched full-length on her sleeping bag and half-turned her head so that she looked directly at Kane. Their mouths were only three or four inches apart.

'I can't do anything at the moment, I'm not armed,' he said. 'How are they treating you?'

'So far, all right, but I'm not happy about the way Selim stares at Ruth. He looks as if he has the worst of all possible intentions.'

Kane tried to sound reassuring. 'We'll have to do something about that. I've got to rejoin the others now. Whatever happens, don't worry. With any luck we should be back here in an hour to get you out.' He started to move away and paused. 'Tell Ruth her husband is fit and well.'

Marie's hand slid under the edge of the tent and caressed his face gently. Her eyes were like dark water, full of dangerous currents that seemed to draw him in. He raised the edge of the tent a little more and she pushed her face towards him until their lips met. It was no kiss of passion – it was the kiss of a woman who loves deeply and tenderly, with every fibre of her being. For a moment, his hand tightened over hers and then he moved away quickly.

As he advanced cautiously through the trees towards the well-shaft, he heard someone coming towards him. He dropped flat on his face behind a tree and waited. One of the men he had seen earlier walked past him, so close that Kane could have touched the hem of his robe.

When he reached the edge of the trees, he could see the remaining Bedouin standing by the mouth of the shaft. The man had no rifle, and Kane waited until he turned to look along the valley, and moved soundlessly across the sand.

The Bedouin stood no chance. One arm encircled his throat, effectively choking back his cry of fear as Kane relentlessly applied pressure. For a moment or two, the man struggled and then his body went limp. Kane dragged him across to the trees and left him lying in the shadows.

The rope was still lying coiled by the tree to which it

was attached. Kane tossed it down the shaft and called softly, 'Get up here as fast as you can.'

He waited, eyes anxiously probing the trees towards the camp. Within a few moments, Cunningham was by his side and then Jamal.

They moved into the trees and Kane quickly explained the situation.

'The two women are under guard in one of the tents. The way I see it, there isn't much point in trying to take over the camp without weapons. I suggest we make for the cave where Skiros stores his arms. There's also a radio there. If we can't raise Mukalla or Aden, we can probably reach Jordan.'

'Sounds like the most sensible course to me,' Cunningham said.

Kane explained rapidly to Jamal in Arabic, and moved off through the trees towards the encampment. They skirted the fire, round which most of the Bedouins were still singing and dancing, and crawled through the camp, keeping close to the ground.

As they passed the rear of the largest tent, Kane paused as Muller's voice sounded clearly on the night air. He touched Cunningham lightly on one shoulder and moved closer to the tent.

Skiros was speaking now and he sounded pleased with himself. 'I'm glad I got in touch with headquarters on the radio,' he said. 'It was fortunate also that I was able to contact Romero. They'll arrive tonight.'

'But I can't see the point,' Muller said.

Skiros sighed. 'You are really incredibly stupid, Muller. Our work here is finished. As I told Kane earlier, I'm sure we're safe for a month at least, but life has a perverse habit of playing strange tricks on a man. That's why we're going to take this unique opportunity of flying out in the Catalina with Romero. We'll all go to Egypt together, Muller. Cheer up. You'll be part of history.'

'What about the prisoners?' Selim interrupted.

Kane could almost see the indifferent smile on Skiros's fat face. 'I'll leave you to take care of the men. The women will go with us in the Catalina.'

'But you promised the Cunningham woman to me,' Selim said angrily.

'I've changed my mind since then,' Skiros said and his voice was cold. 'Don't let us forget who is running things here. You can find yourself another woman.'

'What will happen to them?' Muller said.

'I really couldn't say,' Skiros told him. 'I look upon the Perret woman as a personal challenge. Making her see reason will be a pleasure.'

Somewhere in the distance a faint humming sounded on the night air and Skiros got to his feet. 'There is the plane, gentlemen. Right on time. Take the women down to the truck, Selim. Muller and I will join you there.'

Cunningham moved suddenly, but Kane grabbed him by the shoulder, pulled him back to the ground. 'Don't be a damned fool,' he whispered into his ear.

They crawled out through the encampment and melted into the shadows. As Kane led the way up the steep slope to the base of the cliff, Cunninham said, 'What the hell are we going to do now?'

'There's only one thing we can do,' Kane told him. 'Stop that plane, but we've got to move fast.'

They walked quietly along the stone ramp and cautiously approached the mouth of the cave which contained the arms. A lone Arab lounged against the rock, rifle carelessly slung over his back. He was singing a sad, monotonous herding song, his eyes staring up at the stars.

Kane pressed Jamal on the shoulder and the huge Somali moved silently. The song ended abruptly on a high note. There was a sudden cracking sound as if a dry branch had been snapped and Jamal lowered the dead man to the ground.

The cave was in darkness and Kane struck a match as he led the way in. There was a large spot lamp standing on top of the radio and he quickly switched it on and turned to the cases of arms.

There were only a few left. The first two he examined were packed with rifles, but the third contained submachine guns. A further search disclosed a box filled with circular, hundred-round clips. Kane handed Cunningham and the Somali two clips each.

'What about the radio?' Cunningham said.

Kane shook his head as he loaded his weapon. 'No time for that now.'

As they went outside, there was the sound of an engine, and a truck moved away towards the temple and the outlet to the desert. Kane cursed and started to run down the slope.

Most of the Bedouins were still gathered around the fire and he moved quickly through the shadows towards the other end of the encampment.

The truck in which they had arrived that morning was standing on the edge of the tents in brilliant moonlight. He said quietly to Cunningham, 'She's ours. You take the wheel and drive like you've never driven before.'

They moved out of the shadows and scrambled in. As Cunningham pressed the starter, there was a sudden shrill cry from behind. Kane turned as several Bedouins ran forward. He raised his sub-machine gun and fired a quick burst and they scattered into the darkness. At the same moment, Cunningham took the truck away on a burst of speed.

As they topped the rise in front of the temple and hurtled towards the entrance to the gorge, the Catalina roared overhead, undercarriage and flaps down as it pointed for a landing on the flat plain outside.

'Give it everything you've got,' Kane cried, and Cunningham pressed his foot flat on the boards. The truck bounced over the rock-strewn surface of the valley and he fought for control, and then they were out in the open and chasing the plane.

Over on their right and clearly visible in the moonlight was the other truck. As they approached, Kane could clearly see Selim sitting in the rear, Skiros and Muller in front.

Skiros's face was contorted with anger and he shouted something over his shoulder to the Arab. As they drew abreast, Selim raised a rifle and fired. Skiros swung the other truck towards them and Selim fired again. Kane ducked as the windscreen shattered, and Cunningham jerked the wheel desperately to one side and they skidded round in a complete circle.

For the moment they were safe and able to concentrate on the plane which was starting to touch down. As Romero applied his brakes, dust and sand rose into the night in a great cloud.

Sitting in the second pilot's seat Noval turned and grabbed Romero's shoulder. 'There's a firefight going on out there. Let's get out of here.'

'Give me a chance, for God's sake,' Romero said and boosted power.

Kane glanced back and saw that the other truck was overtaking them fast, and Cunningham swung the wheel in a half-circle that took them into the centre of the great dust cloud that was the plane's wake.

For several moments they drove blind, choking and coughing, heads lowered against the stinging particles, and then the Englishman swung the wheel again and they shot out into the moonlight.

The Catalina was now taxi-ing towards the valley entrance at twenty or thirty miles an hour. Cunningham jerked the wheel, spinning the truck and a moment later they were driving on a parallel course.

Cunningham moved closer and Kane and Jamal stood up and started to pour a concentrated fire into the plane at point-blank range. Kane could see Romero high up in the nose of the aircraft, the dim light from the instrument panel illuminating his face. He raised his sub-machine gun and fired several times into the cabin. Romero ducked out of sight and the tail of the plane slewed round in a great arc, throwing a cloud of sand into the air.

Cunningham spun the wheel in a reflex action that took them out of harm's way as the plane turned completely round and started to move out into the desert again, the engine note deepening as Romero prepared to take off.

And then the entire aircraft seemed to shake from side to side and slewed violently to the left. A moment later, it lurched forward on to its nose and ploughed into the sand for about a hundred yards before coming to rest in a mass of twisted metal, orange tongues of flame leaping upwards into the night.

There was an explosion, followed by another, as the tanks went up. Cunningham turned the wheel quickly, turning away as fingers of flame reached out to touch them and pieces of twisted metal hummed through the air.

The other truck was moving fast towards the gorge and they gave chase, bounding over the ground like some living thing. Kane stood with one foot on the running board, his eyes never leaving the tail-light of the other vehicle, sub-machine gun ready.

As they passed into the gorge, the truck bounced high into the air as it lifted over a slight rise in the ground, and he was swung violently sideways. The sub-machine gun went flying into the night, as he crashed into the soft sand and rolled over and over.

As the truck braked to a halt thirty or forty yards away, it came under heavy fire, and Kane saw several Bedouins appear from behind the jumbled boulders which, at this point, fringed the bottom of the cliffs.

He could hear the bullets thudding into the body of the truck and he scrambled to his feet and cried, 'Get to hell out of here, Cunningham! Get the women!'

The truck moved away at once and Kane crouched low, searching desperately for his sub-machine gun. He saw it lying in a patch of moonlight and ran forward to retrieve it. There was a complete silence for a moment or two and then a stone rattled. He fired into the night. He threw himself behind a boulder as several shots replied, whining through the air above his head and ricocheting from the cliffs. As they finished, he slipped behind the boulder and, keeping to the shadows, ran along the valley.

Behind him, they still fired blindly, but for the moment, he was alone. He ran along the great avenue which led to the temple, crossed in front of it and continued towards the oasis.

When he reached the rim of the hollow, he paused and looked down into the encampment. Cunningham had halted the truck some twenty or thirty yards away from the tents and he and Jamal were sheltering behind it.

Several Bedouins were moving higher up the slope on their right with the obvious intent of being able to shoot down on them. As Kane was about to shout a warning, Cunningham looked up and saw the danger. He tapped Jamal on the shoulder and they turned and scrambled up the slope towards the cave where the arms were, keeping in the shadows.

For the moment, they had not been seen and Skiros was not aware of their departure. There was a short period of silence and Kane started to work his way diagonally up the slope.

He paused behind a boulder and looked up. As Cunningham and the Somali reached the ledge, several Yemenis breasted the slope, cutting them off. Cunningham fired a long burst to keep their heads down, and he and Jamal turned and ran for the shelter of the other cave. Kane slipped from behind the boulder and scrambled up the slope to join them, praying the shadows would hide him.

From the valley below he heard a cry of anger from Selim, and immediately afterwards, heavy firing commenced. He was gasping for breath and he hugged the sub-machine gun tightly to his chest with one hand and clawed at the loose soil with the other. He could hear the roars of men behind him as they started to follow and then there was a long, continuous roll of thunder above his head. He looked up to see Cunningham crouched on the ledge, sub-machine gun to his shoulder.

Kane fell forward on to his face and Jamal's strong hands lifted him and dragged him towards the cave. They stumbled inside and Cunningham crouched at the entrance, his face clearly illuminated by a broad tracer of moonlight which streamed through, touching the entrance to the passage.

'That was a pretty close-run thing,' Kane said after a while.

Cunningham nodded. 'We couldn't pour it in hot and

strong down there. I was frightened we might hit the women.'

Kane nodded. 'That's his trump card and Skiros knows it.'

Several bullets whined through the entrance and spattered against the cave wall and he looked out cautiously. The floor of the valley was dappled with moonlight, and the enemy were clearly visible as they advanced from boulder to boulder.

'Wait until they're half-way up the slope and fire when I give the order,' Kane said.

They waited in silence. Skiros was in the lead and once he looked up towards them, the moonlight falling clearly on his face. Kane grunted. 'I'll say this for the bastard. He's got guts.'

And then Skiros had reached the large boulder splashed with moonlight which Kane had chosen as the half-way mark. 'Now!' he said, and pressed the trigger.

The three guns chattered in unison and there were screams and cries of dismay from below as several Arabs rolled down the slope to the floor of the valley.

The rest of them retreated fast, followed by Skiros, cursing at the top of his voice in German.

In the silence which followed, Cunningham sighed deeply. 'Well, that looks like that for the moment.'

Kane shook his head. 'He isn't going to put up with

much of this. I've a feeling he'll come up with something nasty at any moment.'

As he spoke, Skiros walked forward. 'Kane,' he called. 'I'm not going to waste words on you. I'll give you fifteen minutes to come down with your hands up. If you don't, something unpleasant will happen to the ladies. I'm sure you and Cunningham don't want that.'

Kane touched Jamal on the shoulder and the three of them got up and moved back from the entrance. 'He's got us cold,' Cunningham said. 'We can't let him hurt the women.'

Kane shook his head and his eyes were grim. 'If he wants to harm them, he will and nothing we do will have any effect on him.' He shook his head. 'I think he's stalling. He's probably got some scheme cooking.'

At that moment there was a movement high up on the face of the cliff outside and the stones rattled down on to the ledge in a fine spray.

'I told you the bastard had something up his sleeve.' Kane said, and then a grenade rolled inside the entrance of the cave, clearly visible in the patch of moonlight.

He turned, pushing Cunningham and the Somali violently backwards into the narrow entrance of the tomb and followed them, dropping to his hands and knees.

The grenade exploded, bringing down a shower of stones into the entrance, then the whole cliff seemed to tremble and the roof started to cave in.

Muller stared up at the cloud of dust clear in the moonlight. 'Oh my God. Now what?'

'We get the hell out of here,' Skiros said. 'Back to Dahrein. Leave on Selim's dhow. At least that bastard Kane and his friends have had it. I hope he takes a long time to die entombed in there.'

'But Berlin, the Führer? What will happen to us?'

'Nothing, you fool. I'll get straight on the radio; tell Ritter the Catalina crashed. Hardly our fault and all they need to know.'

'And the women?'

'They can come with us for the time being. Now pull yourself together and let's get moving.'

He turned and went back down to the camp, waving Selim and the remaining Bedouins to follow him.

In Berlin, Canaris was standing at the window of his office having a cognac when there was a knock on the door and Ritter entered. The young major was pale and obviously disturbed.

'Bad news, Hans?'

'Operation Sheba, Herr Admiral. I've had a rather garbled message from Skiros. He's closing down and getting out. There was trouble of some sort, the Catalina destroyed, Romero and his men dead.'

'How very unfortunate,' Canaris said.

'But the Führer, Herr Admiral. What will he say?'

'The Führer, Hans, has a tendency to be very excited about something on Monday, which he has totally forgotten about by Friday.' Canaris smiled. 'And after all, he still has Poland.'

'Can you be certain he'll react in this way?' Ritter said.

'Of course. I've had considerable experience as regards the Führer's mental processes, Hans.'

Canaris went and got another glass. 'Here, have a cognac. When you've been in this game as long as I have, you learn to take the rough with the smooth.'

'If you say so, Herr Admiral.'

'Oh, but I do.' Canaris raised his glass. 'To the Third Reich, Hans, and may it last a thousand years.' He laughed. 'And if you believe that, you'll believe anything.'

THIRTEEN

THE CAVE WAS in complete darkness and Kane took out the small book of matches he had last used in the shaft. There were only three left and he struck one with fingers that trembled slightly.

The small tongue of flame flowered outwards, picking Cunningham's sweating face from the darkness. The Englishman laughed shakily. 'What happens now?'

'Let's have some light on the situation,' Kane said. 'Didn't you leave the tools and a spot-lamp at this end of the passage when we finished work?'

The match burned down to his finger and he dropped it and lit another. He squatted, holding the match at arm's length, and Cunningham said, 'Got it!'

A moment later, a powerful beam of hard white light flooded across to the other side of the cave, slicing the darkness in two. The cave had decreased in size by at least a half, and a sloping bank of rubble and stones lifted backwards, completely blocking the entrance.

It was unpleasantly warm and the air was heavy with settling dust and the acrid tang of explosives. 'Well, what's our next move?' Cunningham said.

Kane started to take off his shirt. 'I should have thought that was sufficiently obvious. We've got to dig and keep on digging. At least we've got the tools, which is something.'

'And what about our friends outside?'

'As far as they're concerned, we're dead meat,' Kane said. 'They probably think the damned mountain came in on us.'

'They wouldn't be far wrong either,' Cunningham told him. He flashed the spot up to the roof and around the walls. 'The whole place still looks damned shaky to me.'

Kane took the spot from him and set it down on the floor so that the beam rested upon the rock-filled entrance. 'The only thing we've got to worry about is the battery in this spot-lamp. You'd better pray that it holds out long enough.'

But there was more to worry about – much more. They laboured feverishly in the weird, dust-filled light, stripped to their waists, sweat pouring freely from their naked bodies.

Jamal was a tower of strength, his great hands lifting, unaided, rocks which Kane and Cunningham could not have moved together. Time ceased to have any meaning as they worked on, fingers bruised and raw. Finally, Jamal, who was working a little in advance of Kane, gave a strange, animal moan and moved backwards.

'What is it?' Kane demanded in Arabic.

The Somali turned, the whites of his eyes shining in the light of the lamp. He pointed and Kane crawled forward into the narrow cutting they had cleared into the heart of the rockfall.

The beam from the spot picked out an immense slab of stone weighing at least three or four tons, which stretched across their path, firmly wedged into place with rocks of varying sizes.

Cunningham crouched at his shoulder and whistled softly. 'My God, we haven't a hope in hell of moving that thing.'

He had stated the obvious and there was no answer. They moved back slowly and slumped down against the wall beside the entrance to the passage.

Kane sat looking at the beam of the spot for a moment and then he leaned down and switched it off. 'No sense in wasting the battery.'

Cunningham laughed lightly and Kane knew that he was near to breaking-point. 'It's damned warm in here. I wish I had a cigarette.'

Neither of them had put it into words and yet it lay between them like a sword. The unspoken, undeniable fact that they were finished. That there was no hope left.

The darkness settled upon them with a weightless pressure. Something seemed to move through it in a soundless wave and a strange, sibilant whispering echoed through the cave as if someone had sighed and the sounds were moving on for ever like the ripples in a pool.

Kane shivered and pushed the thought away from him. It was unhealthy to give way to despair too soon. He had to keep his mind active. He had to think of something other than this box of darkness.

He started to think about the past, letting his thoughts drift back, examining each milestone in his life, the good and the bad.

Only once before had he been in such a hopeless position. Second pilot on an Army Air Corps DC3 flying to Guam in the Pacific. They'd come down in the Pacific, ten people, including passengers, and one life-raft. Sharks nosing around within an hour. By the third day they were down to four, by the seventh day two, and just when he'd thought he was about to die there'd been a droning noise in the sky. He'd looked up and there it was, a Catalina coming in to land. Twice in his life Catalinas had been significant. One had saved him, the other he had destroyed.

And then home. He remembered that first day, flying into La Guardia and seeing New York again. But where was home? Was it an apartment overlooking Central

Park? Was it his father's farm in Connecticut? It was neither of these places. It did not exist in fact, but only in the heart, and he had searched for a long time, never finding, always seeking.

Marie's face seemed to flame out of the darkness at him and he laughed softly. At least one good thing had come out of all this. He knew now that she was important to him – more important than anything in his life. The thought of her was warm and comforting, rather like the kiss she had given him earlier, but he would never be able to tell her these things now.

He got to his feet to stretch his aching limbs, and a cold finger of air from the passage touched his flesh, and he shivered.

It was a moment before its exact significance struck home and he dropped on his knees and searched in the darkness for the lamp. Cunningham blinked in the sudden glare. 'What's the matter?'

'There's a current of cold air blowing from the tunnel,' Kane told him.

Cunningham frowned. 'That's impossible. Where could it come from?'

'There's only one way to find out,' Kane said.

He explained the situation to Jamal in Arabic and then followed Cunningham along the passage to the spot where they had finished work earlier in the day.

The Englishman dropped to his knees in front of the

pile of rubble and stone that blocked the passage and cried out at once, 'You're right, Kane, I can feel cold air on my body.'

Kane dropped down beside him and was at once aware of the pressure of air against his bare chest. 'One thing's for sure,' he said. 'Muller was wrong. Whatever else it might be, this isn't the entrance into a rock tomb.'

'Then where the hell does it lead?' Cunningham demanded.

Kane grinned. 'To a better hole than this – that's for certain.'

Jamal had gone for the tools and now he returned, and Kane and Cunningham started to dig. The space was confined and, after a while, the Somali pulled them out of the way to manhandle a large stone with his bare hands. A hole appeared and air came through in a sudden rush. Jamal carefully lifted several other stones out of the way and then he was on his belly and crawling forward. Kane held the spot on him and he and Cunningham watched the Somali vanish.

After a short time his head appeared and his mouth opened in a huge grin. He beckoned to them and Cunningham dropped to his stomach and crawled forward, followed by Kane.

On the other side of the barrier of stones, the passage was clear, but the roof was considerably lower and they had to walk bent double. Kane followed the Englishman closely, holding the spot-lamp extended in front of him.

They came to the end of the tunnel and crawled out on a shelving bank of shale. It sloped steeply down for fifty or sixty feet into the dark, swirling waters of a river that welled up from the base of the cave and flowed out through a narrow gap between rocks.

Kane swung the spot-lamp in an arc. The roof was shrouded in darkness and must have been of great height, and the stone walls were black and grim and sweated moisture.

Cunningham squatted on his haunches, heels digging into the loose shale. 'There doesn't seem a great deal of choice, does there?'

'That about sums the situation up,' Kane told him. 'You wait here and I'll go back for the guns.'

When he returned, Jamal and the Englishman were at the water's edge, and as Kane slithered cautiously down the steep bank, the Somali backed slowly into the river, Cunningham grasping both his hands.

The water rose to his waist and then stopped. He advanced carefully, hands extended in front of him. After touching the opposite wall with his fingertips, he waded back, a broad grin on his face.

Cunningham laughed excitedly. 'It looks as if our luck's beginning to turn.'

'Let's hope so,' Kane said.

He distributed the guns and gave Jamal the spot-lamp. The Somali led the way and he and Cunningham slipped down into the water and followed.

It was bitterly cold, and after a while the water lifted to Kane's armpits. At first he held the sub-machine gun high above his head, but soon his arms began to ache with the effort and he slung it over one shoulder, allowing it to dangle in the river.

Gradually the current increased in force, as the gap through which the river was running narrowed. He was only a foot or so behind Cunningham and he could see Jamal in front holding the spot-lamp high out of the water.

The roof seemed to come down to meet him and he realized that it was only two or three feet above his head. He pushed furiously as the current lifted him and then he seemed to slide downwards in a rush and the water covered his head.

His feet touched bottom and he kicked upwards, then he surfaced to the light shining in his eyes and his knees banged against a gently sloping bank of shale.

He stayed there for a moment, his chest heaving painfully. After a time, he realized that Cunningham lay beside him, and Jamal gave them a hand up and they stood knee-deep in water, shivering in the intense cold.

The river had emptied into a large round pool, and

the only apparent exit, a narrow slot in the rock, was
blocked by a wall of dressed stones, which stood some
three feet above the surface of the water.

'This looks as if it's been here a hell of a long time,'
Cunningham said.

Kane nodded. 'But what purpose does it serve, that's
the question.'

He took the spot-light from Jamal and pulled himself
up on top. The wall was perhaps ten feet high, and
water oozed through numerous cracks and ran down a
steep incline, the sound of it echoing through the
darkness.

'This must have been the route the river followed
originally,' Kane said. 'The wall was placed here to
change its direction.'

He shone the lamp down on the dark waters of the
pool. That means they must have constructed an artificial
exit for this lot.'

'But why?' Cunningham said.

'God knows. The reason isn't important now, but
finding a way out of this place is.' Kane placed his sub-
machine gun on the wall and gave Cunningham the
lamp. 'Let me have as much light as you can. I'm going
down to take a look.'

He dropped into the water, took a deep breath and
went under. The pool was about ten feet deep, and the
light from the spot-lamp filtering down enabled him to

find what he was looking for almost at once. It was the entrance to a low arched tunnel some four feet high.

He pulled himself in and went forward, his fingers brushed against the smooth, slimy sides, and then it was dark, utterly dark and he turned in a panic and swam back towards the faint light of the lamp and surfaced, rasping for air.

'What's it like?' Cunningham demanded.

Kane waded out of the water and stood knee-deep on the bank of shale beside the wall. 'Bloody murder. There's a tunnel that's hardly big enough to crawl through. I swam along it for a few yards, but it didn't seem to be getting anywhere.'

He pulled himself up on to the wall and Cunningham turned the beam of the lamp into the slot below. 'Once again we don't seem to have a great deal of choice, do we?'

Climbing down presented no problem. There were plenty of footholds where the mortar between blocks of stone had crumbled away, leaving a score of deep cracks through which water trickled steadily.

The steeply inclined floor of the slot was slimy and treacherous to the feet, and Kane led the way cautiously for some fifty yards, until the roof closed in on them and they were faced with a dark opening.

They moved inside and stood ankle-deep in water, and he flashed the lamp from side to side. As the beam splayed across smooth walls, thousands of tiny chisel marks sprang into view.

'The river must have created this passage in the first place,' Cunningham observed, 'but someone's certainly done a hell of a lot of work on it since.'

Kane moved forward slowly, a strange excitement stirring inside him. The sound of the river faded behind them and they were alone in a dark and mysterious world.

The passage twisted and turned, moving down all the time, and the water gradually deepened. As they rounded a corner, they came to an off-shoot at one side.

Cunningham glanced at Kane enquiringly and Kane shrugged. 'May as well take a look.'

They moved into a room about ten feet square, with walls of drafted masonry. Great store-jars, each almost as tall as a man, stood like silent sentinels on either side.

'Grain jars,' Kane said.

As he turned away, the beam of the lamp fell across the far wall and figures leapt to life in vivid colour.

The painting depicted some ancient triumph. Prisoners, most of whom seemed to have short, curling beards, moved together in a column, legs shackled, backs bowed against the whips brandished by soldiers in fish-tailed breastplates and helmets.

'My God,' Cunningham said. 'Have you ever seen anything like it?'

'Only in the Nile Valley,' Kane told him. 'Certainly not in Arabia.'

They moved out into the passage and continued past several other store rooms, finally coming into a wider, pillared passage, the walls of which were covered with paintings.

At one point Kane halted beside a nook inside which stood several clay jars with painted sides. As he lifted one down to examine it, Cunningham moved forward excitedly. 'They're funeral urns, aren't they?'

Kane nodded. 'The whole thing's beginning to click into place. Those grain jars and now these. Offerings to the gods for a safe journey. We must be coming to a tomb.'

He lifted the round lid of the jar and looked inside. It was empty. 'Probably oil or spices or something like that – gone with the years.'

Cunningham took down another jar which also proved to be empty. Kane was about to turn away when he noticed a smaller one, the top held in place by clay seals, standing on a small shelf at the back of the nook.

He put down the lamp with one hand and lifted the jar with the other. As he stepped back, it slipped from his fingers and smashed against the stone floor of the passage.

He lifted the lamp, and as he directed the beam on the

floor, there was a glint of gold amongst the sharded pieces of clay and a flash of green fire.

He dropped to one knee and carefully picked it up. It was a beautiful gold necklace and pendant. Carefully set in the gold filigree were three perfect emeralds, sparkling in the lamplight.

Cunningham whistled softly. 'They'd give their eye-teeth to have *that* in the British Museum.'

Kane took out his handkerchief and wrapped it carefully about the necklace, knotting the ends before placing it in his pocket.

He picked up the lamp again. 'I've an idea there's more up ahead. Much more.'

He moved on quickly and they descended a short flight of steps and faced a bronze door. By now the water was thigh-deep, and Cunningham waded forward to lift the locking bar and he and Jamal pulled the heavy door slowly outwards.

The bronze swing pins were set in holes drilled in the solid rock, and the door swung open effortlessly with a slight, eerie cracking sound.

For a moment Kane stood there, a wave of greyness sweeping through him as if by instinct he knew that they were on the verge of something tremendous, and then Cunningham pushed him forward impatiently.

FOURTEEN

THEY ENTERED A LARGE chamber which was about three feet deep in water. It was otherwise completely empty, but the walls were covered with paintings. Kane swung the beam of the lamp slowly along, carefully examining them, and something jumped out at him with the force of a physical shock.

The particular scene depicted a king standing before his throne at the top of a flight of steps. Around his neck was suspended the Star of David. He was holding out his hands in welcome to a woman who advanced to meet him, her long train carried by twelve maidens.

For a moment, she seemed to float out of the darkness but it was only a trick of the light. She gazed out at him, remote and austere, her beauty fixed for eternity, and he stared back. Above the painting was an inscription in Sabean. He translated it slowly, and when he had finished, the wall seemed to undulate and a strange, quiet whisper rippled through the room as though her voice called to him across time itself.

He stretched out a hand and leaned his head against the cold stonework, and behind him Cunningham said, 'What does it say?'

Kane pulled himself together. 'It says "Solomon the Great King greets Balquis".'

Cunningham seemed to lurch to one side, and Jamal moved in quickly and caught him. In the light of the lamp the Englishman's face looked white and drawn, the eyes suddenly enormous.

'Balquis,' he whispered. 'Queen of Sheba.'

He pulled away from Jamal and moved forward and touched the painted figure very gently with his finger-tips. When he spoke there was awe in his voice. 'A biblical legend and we've brought her to life.'

Kane turned and waded towards the far end of the chamber, and the rays of the lamp picked out another entrance, flanked by carved pillars. In place of a door there was a wall of large dressed stones.

Cunningham moved beside him. 'What do you think?' he said and his voice was strained and unnatural.

'I said there was a strong Egyptian influence here,' Kane told him. 'There must be a stone burial chamber on the other side.'

Cunningham seemed to have difficulty in speaking. He swallowed and said, 'Do you think it might be hers?'

'Anything's possible in this business,' Kane said. 'You know that as well as I do.'

Cunningham nodded several times and turned and looked back towards the wall painting. Waves caused by their movement through the water rippled across the room and splashed against the wall and his breath hissed sharply between his teeth.

He grabbed the lamp from Kane's hand, plunged forward, water foaming around him and dropped to his knees at the base of the painting of Solomon and Balquis.

He gave a cry of anguish. 'The water, Kane. It's spoiling it. Part of the painting's gone already.'

Kane took the lamp from him and pulled him to his feet without saying anything.

'Thank God we've made the discovery when we have,' Cunningham said. 'Another couple of years and that dam back there would have been down and the river flowing in. Everything would have been ruined.'

'I know,' Kane said calmly.

Cunningham laughed wildly. 'For God's sake, man, don't you realize what we've found here? The greatest archaeological discovery ever made. We'll be world-famous.'

'That's hardly likely,' Kane said, 'because the way things look, you may never get the chance to tell any-body about it.'

He turned from the sudden shock on the Englishman's face, gave the lamp to Jamal and they waded towards the door. Cunningham stayed there in the middle of the chamber and they were already moving back along the passage before he started to follow.

As they ducked through the low entrance and climbed the steep incline to the wall that dammed in the pool, Cunningham caught up with Kane and grabbed him by the shoulder.

His face was white and strained, taut with anxiety. 'We've got to get out of here now, Kane. We *must* find a way.'

'Finding a way is simple enough,' Kane said. 'I realize that now. The problem for you will be whether you're willing to take it.'

Jamal quickly climbed the wall and then reached down and pulled them up in turn. Kane took the lamp and played the beam down into the pool and Cunningham said, 'You mean the underwater tunnel? But you said it was impossible.'

'It wouldn't be if there was no water in it,' Kane said.

Cunningham frowned. 'I don't understand.'

'It's really quite simple. We go back up-river for the tools we left in the cave. The wall's already in a pretty shaky state. It wouldn't take us long to demolish enough of it to drain the pool and send the river back on its old course.'

Cunningham still had that slight frown on his face. 'But you must be joking. It would flood the passage and the main chamber, probably even seep into the tomb. Those wall paintings wouldn't last a day under water. They'd be destroyed for ever.'

'I know,' Kane said patiently. 'On the other hand, I can't see that we have a great deal of choice. I'm assuming, of course, that you still have an interest in your wife's welfare.'

Cunningham flinched as if he had received a physical blow. He turned away as Kane continued, 'There's no need for you to come. Jamal and I can manage, but I'm afraid we'll have to take the lamp. I'll try to be as quick as possible.'

'Don't worry about me,' Cunningham said, without turning round. 'I'll be fine.'

For a moment Kane hesitated, wondering whether the Englishman intended to do something silly, and then he shrugged and turned and explained the situation quickly in Arabic to Jamal.

The Somali took the lamp and led the way back up the rock slide and into the dark mouth of the tunnel through which the river emptied into the pool. The journey was not as bad as Kane had thought it would be, except for one or two deeper places where the gap narrowed and the current seemed to be trying to press him back with an implacable hand.

When they reached the steep bank of shale and scrambled up to the mouth of the tunnel which had granted them their freedom from the cave, it had a strangely unfamiliar look like some place visited once and briefly years before and never again.

Kane carried the three picks, and Jamal the hammers and crowbars and they went down the bank and entered the water again.

The return journey seemed only to take minutes and, as Jamal carefully negotiated the slide down into the pool, the beam of the lamp splashed out across the wall. There was no sign of the Englishman.

They dropped the tools quickly, and Kane took the lamp and called, 'Cunningham!'

The sound of his voice rebounded from the narrow walls of the cave but there was no reply. He was about to call out again when there was the sound of a boot on stone in the darkness below. He shone the beam down into the slot and picked out Cunningham coming up the steep incline.

The Englishman looked up at him calmly, shading his eyes against the light. 'You were quicker than I thought.'

'Where the hell have you been?' Kane demanded.

Cunningham turned and looked back down the incline to the entrance to the tunnel. 'I went for another look.'

'Without a light?' Kane said incredulously.

Cunningham smiled and, all at once, the strain seemed to have left his face. 'I couldn't see her, but I knew she was there.' He took a deep breath. 'Down here at the base looks a good place to start. Some of these stones are half-rotten.'

Kane couldn't think of anything to say. He nodded to Jamal and went over the wall, and the Somali passed the tools down to them and they started work.

It took them half an hour to lever out the first stone and Jamal's great strength proved invaluable. The pressure of the water pushed the stone the last few inches like a cork from a bottle, and a great foaming jet splashed out into the slot and rushed down into the darkness below.

Once the gap had been made, the rest was easy. Jamal reached in, water cascading over his back and pulled the next stone away by hand.

Within a moment they were knee-deep in water and Kane turned quickly to Cunningham. 'Now we've made the breach, the whole damned lot might come down. We'd better get back on the other side out of harm's way.'

They climbed over the wall and stood on the bank of shale and sand that had been formed by the years in the corner of the wall and the cave, and gradually the level of the pool dropped.

By now, the river, as it emerged from the slide, was finding its new exit and the wall started to vibrate with the shock. After about half an hour, it sagged in the centre and then cascaded outwards into the slot.

Already the top of the tunnel was showing, and within another ten minutes, there was no more than two feet of water in it. The Somali took the lamp and ducked into the tunnel and Kane slipped the sling of his sub-machine gun over his shoulder and followed.

As he plunged forward into the darkness, water swirling around his knees, he thought of the men who had worked here in the bowels of the earth all those years ago; worked in the darkness, patiently, perhaps for years, that their queen might have a secure resting-place in death.

The river emptied into a wide lake with startling suddenness and he found himself swimming again. Jamal held the lamp high above his head, and its rays picked out a row of carved pillars on the far side and a landing stage.

The Somali reached it first and heaved himself up with easy strength in spite of the fact that the water level of the lake had obviously dropped several feet. He then knelt down and pulled up Kane and Cunningham in turn.

Kane took the lamp and moved forward between the pillars and entered a wide passage which sloped gently upwards. A few moments later, the beam from the lamp splayed itself against a blank wall.

He dropped to one knee and examined it closely. 'From the look of it, this central block pivots,' he said to Cunningham.

He spoke rapidly in Arabic to Jamal and the Somali dropped to his knee and pushed against the great stone wall with all his strength. It refused to budge. The Somali gave a grunt and his back ridged, muscles standing out like cords. Still the stone remained immobile.

Kane dropped to his knees and leaned a shoulder against the stone, and Cunningham moved in on the other side. For a moment, it was as if they were faced with all the power in the world, as if something supernatural was determined they should not leave, and then the stone turned with a groan.

Kane scrambled to his feet and looked about him. They were standing in the temple, and the stone was one of those set in the base of the high altar.

They pushed it back into place, moved outside and stood on the terrace, the morning sun bright in their eyes. The gorge lay still and calm about them and Cunningham frowned. 'It's damned quiet.'

'Most of the Bedouins pulled out with that caravan yesterday afternoon,' Kane reminded him. 'The rest have probably made an early start this morning.'

He led the way cautiously towards the encampment,

using what cover was available. When he neared the edge of the hollow, he got down on his belly and crawled the rest of the way.

The encampment no longer existed. Tents, trucks – everything had gone. For a moment he lay there, a frown on his face, and then Jamal tapped him on the shoulder and pointed beyond the oasis to where a faint tracer of smoke lifted into the morning air.

Kane led the way down into the hollow, unslinging his sub-machine gun. As they neared the trees, a camel coughed and there was the sound of laughter.

On the other side of the oasis, two Bedouin tents still stood with at least a dozen camels hobbled near by. One man squatted before a small fire on which he was cooking, and three more stood knee-deep in the pool and washed themselves.

Kane turned to Cunningham and said quietly, 'You come in from the rear of the tents. Jamal can work his way round to the other side of the pool and I'll go in from here.'

He waited until they were in position and then stepped from behind a tree and went slowly forward. He stopped a yard or so away from the fire. The Bedouin was stirring something in the pot. He laughed, looked up to call to the men washing, and saw Kane. The laughter died in his throat.

'Do as you're told and you won't be harmed,' Kane told him in Arabic.

The man stood up slowly and shrugged. 'I am not a fool.'

He was older than Kane had at first thought, with a fine intelligent face, seamed with wrinkles, and an iron-grey beard. His three companions waded out of the pool to join him, and Jamal and Cunningham moved in behind them.

'Where are the others?' Kane demanded.

'It was thought that you were dead,' the old man said. 'The two Franks and their men left in the trucks before first light. The Yemenis went at dawn.'

'Why have you stayed?'

'We are Rashid,' the old man said simply. 'We do not abandon our kindred. My cousin is lying in one of the tents. You put a bullet in his shoulder last night. One of the Franks removed it before they left.'

'And the women?'

The old man shrugged. 'They went in the trucks.'

Kane turned to Cunningham. 'Did you manage to get all that?'

The Englishman nodded. 'What do we do now?'

'The only thing we can do – get after them.' Kane turned back to the old Rashid. 'You'll have to help us.'

There was a murmur of discontent from the other three, and the old man stilled them by raising a hand. 'Why should we? You are our enemies.'

'Because you haven't any choice,' Kane told them, raising his sub-machine gun. 'After we've eaten, you can select your three best camels, and the Somali is an expert, by the way.'

The old Rashid shrugged. 'As Allah wills it.' His three companions sat down sullenly, legs crossed, and he poured coffee into two battered tin mugs, which he presented courteously to Kane and Cunningham.

Kane drank some of the coffee gratefully and Cunningham said, 'But we haven't a hope in hell of catching them.'

Kane nodded, 'I know, but if we make good time to Bir el Madani and get a truck from Jordan, we stand a good chance of reaching Dahrein before they leave.'

'By God, I hope you're right,' Cunningham said fervently. 'When I think of Ruth . . .' His voice trailed away and he quickly swallowed some coffee.

Kane tried to sound confident. 'You don't have to worry about a thing. Skiros won't be in any hurry to leave Dahrein. There's no reason why he should be.'

But inside he wasn't so sure. Skiros must be a worried man. What else could explain his sudden departure? Perhaps he'd realized that his run of luck was ending, and like a good gambler, was simply getting out while he was still ahead of the game.

Kane narrowed his eyes as he looked up into the blue vault of the sky and watched a buzzard poise before wheeling down in great circles. One could never be sure of anything in this life. If this country had taught him anything, it had taught him that.

FIFTEEN

THEY LEFT AN HOUR LATER on the three camels Jamal considered to be in the best condition. Kane and Cunningham wore the head-dress and loose outer robes of the Bedouin, reluctantly provided by the old Rashid and his companions, and Jamal carried two goatskins of water securely looped over the pommel of his saddle.

Kane was riding a bull camel, a large and powerful black animal which moved across the flat plain outside the gorge at an incredible rate.

Pieces of twisted metal and fuselage from the Catalina were strewn over a wide area, and as they passed the fire-blackened wreckage, he looked at it in wonder. It seemed impossible that they could have destroyed it so completely, and already the memory of the incident had lost its sharpness as if it had never happened.

As they left the plain and entered the sand dunes, he lifted a fold of his head-cloth across his face as a protection against the fierce heat that rose to meet them.

The desert rolled ahead in great waves of sand as far as the eye could see, and he eased himself into a more comfortable position in the wooden saddle and urged the camel on. Speed was the only thing which could help them now. That and the fact that Skiros would not be expecting pursuit.

He glanced back and saw Jamal, close behind, followed by Cunningham, his face half-covered by a fold of his robe. The Englishman raised a hand in a half-salute, and Kane turned and concentrated on the trail ahead.

The camel never faltered in its stride, great legs covering the ground tirelessly, and he lapsed into a state that was somewhere between sleeping and waking, eyes half-closed against the glare.

He wondered what the German's next move would be. He would probably make for Dahrein, secure in the knowledge that no one was left to follow him. He could afford to spend several days there, clearing up his affairs before moving out ahead of any enquiries set on foot by the American Consul.

What he would do with the women was debatable. Kane recalled the conversation he had overheard outside the tent on the previous night. What had Skiros said? That he looked upon Marie Perret as a personal challenge.

Kane shivered at the thought and pushed it firmly away from him. Sufficient unto the day. For the moment it was enough to concentrate on reaching Bir el Madani. He slouched into a more comfortable position in the saddle and urged the camel on.

The morning passed as in a dream and they rolled on into the afternoon like great ships floating over the sand. On several occasions they had to dismount to lead their camels up the steep sides of some of the larger dunes, and they stopped once to share their water and a handful of dried dates.

Cunningham looked tired and his eyes were sore and red-rimmed, the thin, sensitive face coated with sand. Kane swallowed his ration of water, grimacing slightly at the acrid, unpleasant taste, and looked anxiously at him. 'You managing okay?'

Cunningham's face split into a tight grin. 'A little tired, but I'll be fine. Don't forget I passed this way going in the opposite direction.'

They remounted and rode on. The sun was high in the heavens, beating fiercely across their backs with a flail of fire, and Kane bowed his head on his chest and let the camel find its own way. He was tired – very tired. Too much had happened during the past three or four days. Too much for any man.

He decided that he must have ridden unconscious for the rest of the afternoon, because he was suddenly aware that the sun was dropping in the west and a slight wind stung his face. Jamal had ridden up beside him and was pulling at the reins of his camel.

Kane slid to the ground and sat down, shaking his head from side to side to bring himself awake. His mouth was dry as a bone and full of dust and, as Cunningham threw himself wearily down beside him, Jamal produced one of the goatskins and handed it round.

They had two good swallows each and then it was empty. The Somali tossed the useless skin away and walked back to his camel and stood holding its bridle, staring impassively into the distance.

Cunningham's face was drawn and haggard, the skin stretched tightly across the cheekbones. When he spoke, his voice was a dry croak like an old man's. 'What are we going to do – keep going through the night?'

Kane nodded. 'The camels are in good condition. We'll be feeling the shortage of water before they are. We stand a better chance during the cool of the night.'

'What about Skiros?'

Kane shrugged. 'That's another point. He'll probably make camp soon.'

He struggled wearily to his feet, and the wind lifted sand into his face and then Jamal was moving towards him quickly, eyes flashing.

The Somali cupped a hand to one ear in an unmistakable gesture, and Kane listened. Faintly, borne on the wind, came the sound of voices in the distance.

Excitement moved inside him, and the weariness dropped from his shoulders like an old cloak. 'Did you hear it?' he asked Cunningham.

The Englishman nodded. 'Perhaps something went wrong and they've made camp sooner than they intended.'

'Whatever the reason, they're in for one hell of a surprise,' Kane said.

They hobbled the camels and went forward cautiously on foot. The wheel tracks turned away to circle the base of a large dune and Kane hesitated for a moment, and then led the way up the steep side, sinking knee-deep in the soft sand.

He covered the last few feet to the summit on his belly and raised his head cautiously. Seventy or eighty feet below, in a hollow, a tent was standing. A truck was parked beside it, hood raised, while an Arab tinkered with the engine.

As Cunningham moved up, the flap of the tent was thrown back and Ruth Cunningham emerged, pushed by Selim. She seemed to have lost all hope and dragged her feet as she went towards a flaring spirit-stove. She picked up a pan and placed it on the stove, and Selim stood over her, laughing.

Cunningham half-rose to his feet and Kane pulled

him back behind the lip of the dune. 'Don't be a damned fool. At this range, you'd stand as much chance of hitting her as hitting Selim, and if you go down on foot, he'll have her at the other end of his rifle before you get half-way.'

'But we must do something,' Cunningham said desperately. 'We can't afford to wait for darkness.'

Kane's eyes narrowed as he hunted for a solution, and then a quick flare of excitement moved across his face. 'I think I've got it,' he said, and explained rapidly.

When he had finished, Cunningham sat up and nodded slowly. 'It's a good plan. At least it stands an even chance of coming off.'

He started to get to his feet and Kane caught hold of his sleeve. 'I'll handle this. You don't look too good.'

The Englishman shook his head, jaw set firmly. 'She's my wife,' he said simply, 'so it's my job.'

Kane didn't try to argue with him. Cunningham checked the action of his sub-machine gun and slipped it out of sight under his outer robe, holding it with one hand. He smiled once and then pulled back his headcloth and stood up on the summit of the dune.

For a moment, they did not see him, and he opened his mouth and cried hoarsely, 'Water! Water, for the love of God!' He took one deliberate fumbling step forward and fell headlong into the sand, rolling over and over, down into the hollow.

At the first cry, Selim and his companions had turned in alarm, snatching up their rifles. Kane moved cautiously forward and peered down into the hollow as Cunningham rolled to a halt. For a little while he lay there and then he climbed painfully to his feet and lurched forward. 'Water!' he moaned, and pitched forward on to his face.

Ruth Cunningham sprang to her feet. For a moment she stood there, unbelief on her face, and then she started forward. Selim grabbed her by the shoulder and hustled her across to the tent. He pushed her inside and turned.

Cunningham got to his knees and stretched out a hand appealingly and Selim laughed. He shouted something unintelligible to his companion, put down his rifle, and walked forward.

Cunningham stood up and produced the sub-machine gun, and as Selim turned to run, a long burst caught him full in the back.

The other man still stood in front of the truck, rifle in hands. He raised it to his hip and fired one shot wildly. Cunningham swung towards him, a line of bullets lifting the sand in a curtain, driving the man back against the vehicle.

He stopped firing and walked forward until he was standing over Selim, and then the tent flap was thrown back and Ruth emerged and came into his arms.

Kane got to his feet and stood on top of the dune looking at them and a gust of wind drove sand particles against his face. He ploughed down the hill into the hollow, followed by Jamal.

Cunningham held his wife close and she started to tremble as reaction set in. 'It's all right,' he said. 'He can't hurt you any more.'

Selim was dead, fingers clawing into the sand, and Kane looked down at him without pity. The other man was groaning horribly and Jamal knelt beside him and raised his head. As Kane went forward, the man seemed to choke and blood poured from his mouth. His head lolled back and Jamal lowered him to the ground.

'Is he dead?' Kane said.

The Somali nodded and pointed silently at the truck. Along the side facing them, was a neat line of bullet holes. They had emptied the jerrycan of water that was bracketed to the side of the vehicle, and when Kane examined the engine, he found it damaged beyond repair.

He moved back to Cunningham and his wife. 'That final burst of yours caught the truck as well. I'm afraid we'll still have to rely on the camels to get us out of here. How do you feel?'

Cunningham looked pale, but he managed a smile. 'A lot better now that Ruth's safe.'

The wind was increasing, driving the sand across the hollow, and whining round the truck. Kane slung his sub-machine gun over his shoulder, and said quickly,

'Looks as if we're in for some bad weather. You two get into the tent and Jamal and I will get the camels.'

He spoke briefly to the Somali in Arabic and they hurriedly retraced their steps and climbed up the side of the dune. As they moved over the top, the wind lifted in sudden fury, carrying a curtain of sand with it that blotted out everything.

He pulled a fold of his head-cloth about his face and went down the other side of the dune. Already their tracks were obliterated, and within a few moments, they were alone, enveloped in a thick cloud of swirling sand.

It was impossible to see anything. He paused, eyes vainly trying to pierce the gloom, then turned and cannoned into Jamal. He and the Somali linked arms and struggled back up the side of the dune. It was impossible to remain standing on top and they slid down the other side and stumbled blindly into the camp.

Sand was already piled around the base of the tent, and when Kane ducked in through the flap, Ruth Cunningham turned, fear in her eyes. 'How long will it last?' she demanded.

He pulled off his headcloth and tried to sound unconcerned. 'An hour or two. Perhaps a little longer. They always blow themselves out in the end. There's nothing to worry about.'

Jamal carefully laced up the entrance and sat against it, arms folded. Cunningham had an arm round his wife's shoulder and held her close. 'How do you feel?' Kane asked her.

When she spoke, her voice sounded unnatural and strained, like a spring too tightly wound up. 'I never expected to see either of you again. After the fighting last night, Skiros told us you'd been buried under a fall of rock.'

'You'd better bring us up to date,' Kane said. 'What's been happening today and why did the party split up?'

She pushed back a tendril of hair with one hand. 'It was pretty horrible. We left the gorge this morning in the two trucks. Skiros, Muller and Marie in the front one; Selim, his man and myself in the other.'

'Why were you with Selim?' her husband asked.

She flushed. 'Skiros came to some agreement with him. He needed Selim's help when we reached Dahrein. I don't know what it was about, but I was the price Selim demanded.'

There was a short silence. As Cunningham slipped an arm round her shoulders, Kane went on, 'But why the split?'

She shrugged. 'The truck had engine trouble. Selim had to stop to fix it, and Skiros and Muller went on with Marie. They said they'd wait for us at a place called Hazar near Bir el Madani.'

'They'll have to wait a long time for Selim,' Cunningham said.

She looked down at her hands, twisting together nervously in her lap. 'He kept telling me what he was going to do when we camped for the night. He was so loathsome.'

Cunningham pulled her close and she turned her head into his chest and started to cry, her whole body shaking with the violence of her weeping.

Outside, the wind howled, driving the sand against the frail skin of the tent in a relentless fury that was somehow terrifying. Kane bowed his head down on his knees and relaxed, breathing deeply through half-open mouth, feeling each tired muscle ease.

Gradually it became completely dark, and the wind was so violent that he and Jamal had to hang on to the pole at each end of the tent to prevent it from being torn away into the night.

Four hours later, the storm departed as suddenly as it had come, and Kane unlaced the tent flap and crawled outside. The night sky was clear and millions of stars burned in its depths like white candles. The moon was full and its radiance flooded down into the hollow.

The sides of the tent sagged under the weight of the drifting sand and the truck was half-buried. Cunningham ducked out through the opening of the tent and joined him. What do we do now?'

'See if we can round up the camels,' Kane told him. 'I'll take Jamal with me.'

'You don't sound too hopeful,' Cunningham said.

'It was a bad storm. I know we hobbled them, but a frightened camel has surprising strength. Once they get into a panic, they can kick themselves free of anything.'

He called to Jamal and they moved up the steep side of the dune away from the camp. The view from the top was quite spectacular. Rolling dunes stretched away to meet the horizon, and the hollows between them lay dark and forbidding, thrown into relief by the white moonlight, which picked out the higher stretches of ground.

They moved down the other side and walked forward in the general direction of the place where they had left the camels. All tracks had been swept away by the storm, and Kane's heart sank. He stopped and whistled several times, the sound falling shrill on the cold night air, but there was no answering cry.

They separated, Kane going one way, Jamal another, but it was no good. An hour later, they returned to the camp without the camels.

Cunningham was sitting outside the camp, wearing his Bedouin robes against the chill of the night. He rose to meet them, and as they approached, his wife emerged from the tent and joined him.

'No luck,' Kane told them. 'They're probably miles away by now. I'm afraid our last goatskin of water has gone with them as well.'

Cunningham slipped an arm around his wife's shoulders. 'What do we do?'

Kane shrugged. 'There isn't any choice – we start walking.'

'But the nearest water's at Shabwa and that's at least forty miles away,' Cunningham said. 'It's impossible – especially for Ruth.'

Kane went across to the truck, leaned inside the cab and unscrewed the compass from its fixing. When he turned, his face was grim. 'There aren't any ifs or buts about it. We walk, and we walk now. With luck we can cover maybe twenty or twenty-five miles before daylight. If we don't, we're finished.'

Cunningham's shoulders sagged and he turned to his wife. 'In a way, I got you into this. I want you to know that I'm sorry.'

She touched his face gently and smiled. 'There's no place I'd rather be.'

They might have been alone as they stood there, staring into each other's eyes, and Kane turned away quickly and went to speak to Jamal.

SIXTEEN

A THOROUGH SEARCH of the camp produced plenty of food, but only one aluminium water-bottle. When they left at midnight, Kane carried it slung over one shoulder.

Split four ways, its contents were virtually useless, but they had no choice and he was determined it should not be used until the last possible moment.

He led the way at a fast pace, using the compass regularly to check on direction. It was bitterly cold and he felt quite fresh and full of energy. It was ironic to think that, within another six hours, they would be exposed to the merciless rays of the sun. How long they would be able to keep going after that was anyone's guess.

It was the woman who was going to be the problem. He paused to consult the compass again and looked back over his shoulder. Jamal was close behind, with Cunningham and his wife thirty yards in the rear.

Kane started forward again, trying to follow the easy

way through the dunes. On several occasions this proved impossible, and they were forced to toil up the steep side of some sand mountain, every step an effort.

After some two hours, they came out of the dunes and moved down towards a vast flat plain that disappeared into the distance, hard-baked and strewn with gravel. Kane paused to take a bearing, and Jamal came up behind and tapped him on the shoulder. As Kane turned, the Somali pointed back.

Cunningham and his wife were a good two hundred yards away, and Kane sat down in the sand and waited. As they approached, he stood up to meet them, but Ruth Cunningham slipped down to the ground with a heavy sigh. 'I feel as if I've walked twenty miles.'

'I'm afraid we've only done eight or nine at the most,' Kane told her. 'We must cover at least twenty-five before the full heat of the sun hits us or we don't stand a chance.'

'It's all right for you,' Cunningham said, 'but Ruth can't stand the pace. You're going too fast.'

She quickly placed a hand on his arm. 'Gavin is only stating the obvious, John. Don't worry about me. I'll be all right.'

'I know it's tough,' Kane said, 'but it's got to be done.'

Cunningham stood up. 'Well, what are we waiting for?'

It took them almost three hours to cross the plain and they moved rapidly on its hard-baked surface. Ruth Cunningham was doing much better, and when they passed out of the plain and moved into the sand dunes on the other side, they were bunched closely together.

Kane felt no fatigue at all and his long legs, toughened by years of hard living, strode effortlessly over the ground. His mind was not on the present, but on the morning and what it would bring. He pushed the thought away from him and tried to think of other things.

It was then that he remembered that Alexias had done this journey before them and without a compass. He started to go over the manuscript again in his mind, trying to recapture again that vivid image of the man that had come to him after reading it for the first time.

He must have been tough, that much was obvious. Leather and whipcord and an unyielding will. A man who believed in his destiny and in his ability to conquer all obstacles. And yet, were those things enough? There must have been something else. Something which had brought him walking out of the desert on his own two feet when, by all logic, he should have died. A woman, perhaps, waiting for him back home?

It was a question to which there could be no answer and he paused to check on their direction again. It was almost five o'clock, and he sat down and waited for the others to catch up to him.

Ruth Cunningham looked white and drawn in the pale light of the waning moon, and her husband seemed anxious. He gently eased her down beside Kane, and Jamal opened a knapsack and took out dates and boiled rice, which he handed round.

Ruth Cunningham tried to wave her share away, but Kane took it from the Somali and held it out to her. 'You must keep up your strength.'

She smiled wanly and put some of the boiled rice into her mouth. Cunningham said, 'How far do you think we've come?'

Kane shrugged. 'Twenty to twenty-five miles. We made good time across the plain.'

Cunningham looked up into the vast bowl of the sky. 'It seems to be getting lighter.'

'Dawn in an hour,' Kane said. 'We've got perhaps another hour after that before the sun really starts giving us trouble.'

'And then what?'

Kane shrugged. 'We'll worry about that when the time comes.'

He got to his feet and started forward again, and when he glanced back over his shoulder from the top of the next dune, they were trailing close behind him, walking strongly.

They covered another seven or eight miles before the sun slipped up over the edge of the horizon, a blood-red disc whose heat warmed them pleasantly, chasing the cold of the night from their bones.

Kane increased his stride, his eyes on the horizon, watching the sun rise into the heavens with something like despair in his heart. For the first time it occurred to him that it was useless, that what they were attempting was impossible. If they were still walking at noon, it would be a miracle.

The sun was an orange ball of fire and its rays burned their way into his skull. He pulled the ends of the head-cloth across his face, leaving only the eyes free, as a slight breeze lifted dust from the ground.

There was no air to draw into his lungs, only the fiery breath of the sun, searing the flesh and cracking the lips, turning his throat into a dry tunnel of dust.

He began to think about the water-bottle and his fingers went to it. As he plodded on, he looked down at it, imagining the coolness of the water inside, its wetness, the feel of it trickling down his burning throat and spreading throughout his body. He pushed the bottle round to the small of his back where he couldn't see it any longer and started the slow climb up the side of a large sand dune.

When he reached the top, his limbs were tired for the first time and he paused, trembling with effort, feeling the sweat trickling from every pore in his flesh, draining his body of the liquid needed to live.

He shaded his eyes and gazed before him and suddenly he caught a flash of scarlet as the sun sparkled on something in the distance. It was the wrecked Rapide in which he and Ruth had crashed four days previously.

He was filled with a sudden wild hope. The plane had carried a jerrycan filled with water. Allowing for the lapse of time and the great heat, there was still a good chance that some of it remained.

It occurred to him with something of a shock, that he had not checked on his companions for a considerable time. He turned to look back and saw Jamal at the bottom of the sand dune, Ruth Cunningham cradled in his great arms. Cunningham was struggling up the steep slope and his eyes burned feverishly in his swollen face.

He fell on his knees a few feet away from Kane, and passed a hand slowly across his face. Finally, he forced himself upright, and when he spoke, his voice seemed to come from a great distance. 'We've got to rest.'

Kane tried to moisten cracked lips. 'We must keep moving.'

Cunningham shook his head stubbornly. 'Got to rest.' He took a wavering step forward and started to buckle at the knees. As Kane grabbed him, his feet slipped in the soft sand and they went over the edge together, rolling over and over in a cloud of dust to the bottom.

Cunningham lay with limbs sprawled, and Kane dropped to his knees beside him and forced a little water between his teeth. Jamal appeared on top of the dune and moved down to join them. He laid Ruth Cunningham beside her husband and looked at Kane enquiringly.

Kane explained about the plane and something glowed briefly in the Somali's eyes. At that moment Cunningham groaned and sat up. 'Where am I? What happened?'

His voice sounded weak and lifeless as if it didn't really belong to him any more.

Kane lifted him to his feet and slipped an arm around his shoulders. 'Don't worry,' he said soothingly. 'We haven't got far to go now. Not far at all.'

He turned and nodded to Jamal, who picked up the woman again, and they started to walk.

It took them just over an hour to reach the plane, and by the time they were there, Cunningham had become a dead weight on Kane's arm. He lowered the Englishman to the ground and dragged him under the shade of the wing and propped his back against the side of the plane. He left Jamal to handle the woman and climbed into the cabin.

He found the jerrycan with no trouble and his hands were trembling as he carried it out. Something swirled inside so he quickly pulled off the metal stopper and lifted the can to his lips. It tasted terrible, warm and brackish, but it was liquid and there seemed to be four or five pints of the stuff.

He crawled under the wings and poured a little of the water over Ruth Cunningham's face. She groaned and then her eyes opened slowly. The skin was stretched tightly over her flesh and her lips had cracked in several places. He gently raised her head and poured a little water into her mouth.

She coughed and some of it seemed to trickle down her chin, and then she seemed to come alive and her hands reached out for the can, forcing the opening against her lips as she took a long swallow.

She leaned back with a sigh and Kane moved across to Cunningham. The Englishman seemed more himself and managed a weak smile. 'Sorry I was such a nuisance. What happens now?'

Kane indicated the jerrycan. 'You'll find about four pints of water in there,' he said. 'It should keep you going through the rest of the day.'

Cunningham frowned slightly. 'What about you and Jamal?'

'We'll carry on,' Kane said. 'We haven't got any choice. You and your wife can't walk any further. If we stay here with you, we'll all die. If either Jamal or myself gets through, we'll get help to you as soon as possible.'

There was silence for a moment and then the Englishman smiled faintly. 'As you say, there really isn't any choice.' He held out his hand. 'There doesn't seem to be much more I can say except good luck and what the hell are you waiting for?'

For a second longer, they clasped hands, and then Kane moved towards Jamal. He opened the water-bottle and swallowed half its contents. He handed it across to the Somali, who emptied it and tossed it away in one long easy throw. For a moment or two they looked into each other's eyes and then they started to walk. As they topped a small rise, Kane looked back once, and then he took a deep breath and plunged down the other side.

The sun was a living thing that had somehow become a part of him so that they were one, and marched as one. It was impossible to judge how much time had elapsed since they had left the plane, because time had ceased to exist and had no meaning.

A man couldn't walk in breastplate and greaves. It was impossible. Better to discard them. The helmet had gone a long time before and now he marched with only his sword to weigh him down, the short, stabbing sword of the Roman soldier, his riding cloak folded across his head to keep the sun from his brain. He had to keep going, had to get back to the General with his report. Duty came first, as it always must with a soldier, but there was another reason. The girl — the girl with the dark hair and milk-white skin and the mouth that was a cool well. Almost as cool as the sea off the Piraeus at Athens where he had swum as a boy, diving down into the green depths, twisting amongst the fishes, scaring them away in great glittering clouds and rising slowly to the surface in a spiral of bubbles.

He fell forward on his face. For a little while he stayed there on his knees like an animal, and then he was jerked to his feet and a hand slapped him across the face. Jamal held him steady, eyes staring anxiously into his. Kane tried to speak and found that he couldn't. He nodded several times and started forward again.

The effort to march became a physical agony, a pain that blossomed, spreading through his entire body. And then it didn't seem to exist any longer. Now, there was only a small, burning core inside that refused to let him lie down and die.

The wind lifted into his face, blowing aside his head-cloth and the sun cut sharply against the unprotected flesh, and then he was on his face in the sand and Jamal was lifting him again. Later, he was lying across the Somali's broad shoulders, and he frowned and shook his head, trying to think clearly, but it was no good. Nothing was any good now, and he lapsed into a dark vacuum of heat.

There was sand in his mouth and his fingers clawed at the ground, but this time no hand lifted him in its strong grip. This time he was on his own. Utterly and finally alone, and Jamal had gone.

He would never get back to that girl now, the girl with the white limbs and the cool mouth, the girl he had needed all his life to fuse with his being so that they became a single entity, existing together, savouring life to the full in the only way it can be savoured – together.

Was he Gavin Kane or was he Alexias the Greek, centurion of the Tenth Legion, and who was the one with the white arms and the cool mouth? There was no answer. No answer on top of earth.

The water spilled across his face with the shock of a physical blow, trickling down into his mouth, causing him to cough violently. A strong hand raised him and his teeth gripped the metal rim of a water-bottle. He swallowed greedily and doubled over as cramp twisted his guts.

He opened his swollen, red-rimmed eyes and found Jordan supporting him across his knees. In the background a truck was parked.

Kane opened his mouth and managed to speak. 'Back there in the desert,' he croaked. 'Ruth Cunningham and her husband. You'd better get to them quick.'

Jordan nodded reassuringly. 'Don't worry about a thing. It's all been taken care of. Two of my men have already gone for them in my other truck, with the big

Somali to guide them.' He grinned. 'That Jamal is quite a guy.'

But Kane heard no more. His eyes closed as his body twisted in a great shuddering sigh of relief and darkness flooded over him.

SEVENTEEN

HE OPENED HIS EYES slowly. For a moment his mind was a complete blank and he struggled up on one elbow, panic moving inside him, and then he remembered and lay back with an audible sigh of relief.

He was lying on a camp bed underneath a low awning suspended on four poles. Two trucks were parked near by and there was a tent pitched several yards away.

As Kane moved, Jamal, who was squatting at the end of the bed, got to his feel and leaned over him. As their eyes met, a huge smile appeared on the Somali's face, and Kane held out his hand silently.

Jamal took it and the smile faded from his face. For a brief moment, there was a feeling between them that had not existed before, and then he turned away and crossed to Jordan, who was bending over a spirit-stove in the centre of the camp.

Jordan came towards Kane, a pot in one hand and a plastic cup in the other. 'Coffee, sir?' he said with a grin.

Kane swung his legs to the floor and sat on the edge of the bed. He felt curiously weak and light-headed, and somehow, everything was touched with a slight tinge of unreality and blurred at the edges.

He swallowed some of the coffee and shivered as it burned its way down into his stomach. 'I have a feeling I shouldn't really be here.'

Jordan nodded. 'That's putting it mildly.'

Kane peered out from under the awning. They were camped in the foothills of the mountains, and the desert rolled into the distance before them. 'Where are we?'

'About ten or twelve miles from Shabwa,' Jordan answered. 'I made camp here in a hurry because I didn't know what shape Cunningham and his wife were in.'

'How are they?' Kane asked quickly.

Jordan offered him a cigarette. 'Slightly dehydrated, but otherwise okay. I've given them both a sedative. They're asleep in the tent.'

Kane drew the smoke from the cigarette deep into his lungs. 'Lucky for all of us that you met up with Jamal. What were you doing so far out in the desert?'

'I've been looking for you for the past three days,' Jordan said. 'When Marie failed to return in the truck she'd borrowed, the driver waited until the following morning, and then came and told me. I found the plane yesterday, but no sign of the truck. I figured it must have broken down somewhere on the return journey.

We were doing our best to search the area between here and the plane when we came across the Somali.'

Kane glanced across at Jamal, who squatted by the spirit-stove, eating boiled rice from a bowl, closely watched by Jordan's men. 'I guess we owe our lives to him.'

'You can say that again,' Jordan said, 'but how about filling me in on this whole thing? Where have you been since the plane crashed, and what's happened to Marie?'

Briefly and with as much economy as possible, Kane told him of the events of the past four days. When he had finished, Jordan shook his head. 'Skiros a Nazi – it's the most fantastic thing I ever heard.'

'It's true,' Kane said. 'But it's Marie I'm worried about. Ruth Cunningham says they're supposed to be waiting at Hazar.'

Jordan frowned. 'I passed through the place two weeks ago. There's a tribe of Bedouins camped there – Bal Harith. Their chief's called Mahmoud, a wizened old guy with a grey beard.'

Kane nodded. 'I know the man you mean. I've traded with him in the past.' His eyes narrowed. 'Come to think of it, I heard that Muller was pretty thick with the Bal Harith. Maybe he knew they were encamped at Hazar.'

Jordan grinned. 'They're the sort of friends he and Skiros would need. Big, rough-looking guys who bare their teeth and finger their rifles every time I drive by. They'd cut your throat for a pair of socks.'

Kane shook his head. 'Not Mahmoud. He's a Bedouin of the old school. Very keen on his honour and the strict observance of the ancient customs.'

He pushed himself to his feet and walked out from under the awning. He felt light-headed again and swayed slightly, bracing his feet to steady himself. Jordan said anxiously, 'Sure you feel okay?'

'I'll feel a lot better when I catch up with Skiros,' Kane told him. 'Can I borrow one of the trucks?'

Jordan shook his head. 'No need, I'm coming with you. I happen to think quite a lot about Marie Perret myself.'

'What about Cunningham and his wife?'

Jordan shrugged. 'They'll sleep for hours. I'll leave my men here to look after them.'

Kane was too tired to argue. He called Jamal over, explained the situation, and they climbed into one of the trucks and waited for Jordan, who was giving his men their instructions.

They drove away a few minutes later, Jordan behind the wheel, and Kane closed his eyes and leaned back in his seat. It was as if all the action, all the passion of the past few days had finally caught up with him, draining the strength from his very bones. He didn't even bother to think about what lay ahead.

They reached Hazar in just under an hour, and Jordan braked the truck at the head of the wide valley and they looked down on the black tents of the Bedouins.

'Whatever happens, leave the talking to me,' Kane said. 'I know exactly how I'm going to handle it.'

The palm trees of the oasis extended for several hundred yards along the valley, their green fronds forming a solid roof against the rays of the sun. As they drove into the encampment, scattering camels and goats before them, children ran towards the tents with shrill cries of alarm, and tall, black-bearded men in flowing robes emerged, most of them carrying rifles.

As they drove into the centre of the camp, Kane straightened in his seat and Jamal touched him lightly on the shoulder. Fifty or sixty yards away, two trucks were parked.

Jordan saw them in the same moment. 'Looks as if we've come to the right place.'

He braked to a halt outside the largest tent, and a commanding figure moved outside and stood looking towards them.

Mahmoud was very old, his flowing beard heavily streaked with silver, and his skin was drawn tightly like parchment over fine bones. His robes were of dazzling whiteness and the hilt of his *jambiya* was of finely wrought gold.

The tribesmen moved silently in on them, surrounding

the vehicle and effectively cutting off any retreat. They looked anything but friendly.

Jordan said quietly, 'Have you noticed their rifles? The very latest. No wonder Skiros chose to wait here.

Kane got out of the truck, moved forward slowly and halted a few paces away from Mahmoud. For a brief moment they looked into each other's eyes, and then the old Arab smiled and extended his hand. 'My good friend, Kane. It is a long time since we hunted together with the falcons.'

Kane took the proffered hand and smiled. 'Time has been good to you, Mahmoud. Each year you grow younger.' He turned and nodded towards Jordan. 'I bring a friend.'

Mahmoud's face wrinkled with distaste. 'I know him. The young man who tears up the ground and makes the air stink with his machines.' An expression of discomfort appeared on Jordan's face, but the old man smiled and made a courteous gesture with one hand. 'On this occasion we make him welcome for the sake of a friend.'

He turned and walked through the low entrance into the cool interior and Kane and Jordan followed.

They sat cross-legged on soft rugs and waited until a woman shrouded in black robes emerged from the rear of the tent carrying a coffee-pot, three cups, and a bowl of boiled rice on a brass tray.

Kane and Jordan, observing the usual formalities,

drank their coffee and ate a little of the rice, dipping their fingers into the communal bowl as did Mahmoud.

As the woman handed them a damp cloth with which to wipe the grease from their fingers, Kane sighed with relief, all tension easing inside him. Whatever course the conversation took, whatever happened, they were now safe. They had eaten and drunk with Mahmoud in the midst of his tribe. No harm could possibly come to them now.

There was a slight silence before Mahmoud said politely, 'You have come far, my friend?'

Kane nodded. 'Far and fast. I seek two men who have wronged me deeply.'

'A man's honour is his life,' Mahmoud said seriously. 'May Allah guide your footsteps.'

'He has already shown me his great mercy,' Kane replied. 'The men I seek are here in your camp. I have seen their trucks.'

Mahmoud was not visibly moved. He nodded calmly. 'There are two Franks in my tents. My good friend Professor Muller and the fat one from Dahrein. In what way have they offended your honour?'

Kane kept his voice flat and unemotional. 'They have taken my woman.'

There was quiet and the old man stroked his beard gently with one slender hand. After a moment, he said,

'Certainly they have a woman with them. One of mixed blood. She has not left their tent since their arrival.'

'She is the one,' Kane said.

Mahmoud got to his feet with easy grace. 'Wait here,' he said calmly, and went outside.

Jordan moved restlessly. 'What was all that supposed to mean?'

Kane explained quickly. 'It's the one way we can bring Skiros out into the open. A woman may be just a household chattel to a Bedouin, but the similarity ends there. To steal a man's woman is one of the most serious crimes known to these people.'

'Okay, I'll buy that,' Jordan said impatiently. 'But I still don't see how it's going to help.'

Before Kane could reply, Mahmoud came back into the tent, followed by Muller and Skiros.

Kane and Jordan rose to their feet, and Kane moved forward a step. The expression of dismay on Muller's face was ludicrous, but Skiros showed little emotion. 'We saw you arrive. It would appear that miracles still do happen. Presumably Selim has been delayed.'

'Indefinitely, I'm afraid,' Kane replied.

'So, you are old friends,' Mahmoud said softly.

'Hardly that,' Skiros told him. 'This man has done me great harm. One might even say he has also harmed you and your people. Because of his actions, Muller and I must leave the country. There will be no more arms for the border tribes.'

'That is certainly most unfortunate and my people would not be pleased if they knew,' Mahmoud said, 'but Kane is a guest in my tents and his safety is as much my concern as is your own.'

Skiros shrugged. 'Naturally, that is your own affair, but I feel I should warn you that this man is your enemy.'

Mahmoud walked away a few paces as if deep in thought and said slowly, 'This woman you have in your tent, she belongs to you?'

Skiros stiffened and Muller mopped sweat from his face with a trembling hand. 'In what way can this woman concern you?' the German asked.

Mahmoud's voice was quite calm. 'Kane tells me that she is not your woman. That you have stolen her from him.'

Skiros shrugged carelessly. 'I would expect him to say such a thing.'

'I see,' Mahmoud said thoughtfully. 'Two versions of the same affair, each different. Logically, someone must be juggling with the truth. There is one obvious way to find out.'

He clapped his hands and there was a slight movement outside. Marie came through the entrance and stood facing them, blinking her eyes in the gloom, and then she saw Kane. An expression of wonder appeared on her face, and with a slight incredulous cry, she ran into his arms.

He held her close and ran a hand over her dark hair. 'Are you all right?' he said.

'I'm fine – just fine.' She touched his face gently. 'I can't quite believe it.'

Mahmoud placed a hand on her shoulder and turned her round to face him. 'What is your name, child?'

She faced him proudly, chin up-tilted. 'Marie Perret.'

He nodded slowly. 'I have heard of you. Your mother was a Rashid, was she not?' He turned away and stood slightly to one side of the group so that he could see every face clearly. 'This man Kane says that you are his woman. That Skiros has stolen you from him. Is this true?'

She nodded and the old sheik went on. 'Are you married according to the Christian custom?'

'No, we are not married,' she said.

'Has he known you, child?' Mahmoud said gently.

There was a moment of stillness and Kane held his breath, praying that her answer would be the right one. She nodded her head slowly. 'Yes, I have lain with this man.'

Skiros exploded angrily. 'It's a lie. This is a deliberate plot on the part of Kane. I told you he was my enemy.'

Mahmoud stilled him with a raised hand. 'What

woman would shame herself without reason? If she has lain with him, then she is his. She may not belong to another. She is of the blood of my people and it is our law.'

An expression of fury appeared on the German's face, but by a supreme effort of will, he controlled his anger. He bowed stiffly, brushed aside the tent flap, and went out, Muller at his heels.

Jordan emitted an audible sigh of relief and Kane turned to Mahmoud. 'What now?'

The old sheik smiled. 'I think it best if she returns to her tent and stays there under guard until our friends leave.'

'May I speak to her first?' Kane said.

Mahmoud nodded. 'For a little while only.' He touched Jordan on the shoulder and led the way outside, leaving Kane and Marie alone.

She came into his arms and he held her close for a little while, and then they sat down. Kane was suddenly tired – really tired. 'Have you got any cigarettes?' he said.

She took a crumpled pack from her shirt pocket and gave him one. He inhaled and gave a sigh of content. 'That tastes good.'

She reached over and smoothed back his hair. 'You look as if you've been having a pretty thin time.'

'I guess you could call it that.'

'Tell me about it.'

He gave her a brief outline of events, and when he had finished, she gave a sigh of relief. 'I'm glad the Cunninghams are all right. What are you going to do about Skiros and Muller?'

'What can I do? Mahmoud will hold us here after they've left, or I miss my guess. He owes them that much if they've been supplying him with guns. One thing I can't understand is why Skiros decided to leave the valley in such a hurry. What happened?'

'I don't really know,' she said. 'He was on the radio for a long time after the fighting was over. When he came down into the camp, he was very angry. He had a long argument with Selim. Afterwards, he said we'd be leaving at dawn.'

'He was probably in touch with his superiors in Berlin to tell them about the loss of the plane,' Kane said. 'They must have got into a panic. After all, if he was caught and his true nationality disclosed, there'd be hell to pay. They most likely told him to get out – and fast.'

'I hope we never see him again,' Marie said.

Kane held out his hands and she clasped them tightly. 'At least one good thing's come out of all this,' he said. 'I know when I'm licked.'

She came into his arms and they kissed briefly, then the tent flap was thrown back and Mahmoud appeared. He stood to one side and Marie brushed past him.

The old Bedouin smiled. 'You look tired. I suggest a long sleep. I'll have you taken to your friend. We'll talk later.'

Kane went out into the bright sunlight and a man led the way through the encampment. Eyes turned on him curiously and several small children ran at his heels all the way to the tent, which was on the outskirts of the camp. When he ducked in through the entrance, he found Jordan sitting cross-legged on a rug in the centre, eating from a can.

'You look terrible,' the geologist said cheerfully.

Kane managed a tired grin and flung himself down on a sleeping pallet in one corner.

Jordan was still speaking, but the words didn't seem to be making any sense. After a while, they were simply a monotonous drone, and Kane was asleep.

He awakened slowly and lay staring into the gloom. It was night and an oil-lamp hung from the pole above his head, its radiance scattering the shadows from the centre of the tent.

Jordan was sitting near by, cleaning his revolver. As Kane moved, he turned and a smile appeared on his face. 'How do you feel?'

'Out of this world,' Kane said, struggling into a sitting position.

Jordan handed a bowl across. 'You'd better have something to eat.'

Kane pushed balls of boiled rice and pieces of goatmeat into his mouth and discovered he was hungry. 'Has anything been happening?'

Jordan shook his head. 'Quiet as the grave. You've been lying there for about eight hours.'

'Have our friends left yet?'

'They were on the other side of the camp. I suppose the old boy arranged it that way. I heard them drive off a couple of hours ago. What do you think they'll do?'

Kane shrugged. 'Make straight for Dahrein, hoping to get clear before we notify the authorities.'

'Are you going to try to stop them?'

Kane shook his head. 'I don't think so. I'll be glad to see the back of both of them. They're finished round here, anyway.' He got to his feet and stretched. 'Let's call on Mahmoud.'

He brushed back the entrance flap, walked out into the cool night and led the way down through the quiet camp to Mahmoud's tent.

They found the old sheik sitting cross-legged on a sheepskin before the fire, smoking a Turkish cigarette, eyes boring into the heat of the flames.

He greeted them with a smile. 'So, you have recovered, my friend,' he said to Kane.

Kane sat down beside him. 'I understand Skiros and Muller have left?'

The old man nodded. 'I promised them I would hold you here for a day. I owed them that much at least.'

'Skiros was a German,' Kane said. 'Was it wise to have dealings with such a man?'

Mahmoud smiled. 'Your friend represents an American oil company. If he finds oil, how long will it be before we receive the benefits of so-called American aid?'

'Would that be such a bad thing?' Jordan said.

Mahmoud shrugged. 'In Oman, they have the British to protect them. Here, we would rather protect ourselves. If the Germans are foolish enough to give us arms free, I will accept.'

'But most of the border tribes have used those arms to attack the British in Oman,' Kane said. 'This is what the Germans wish to see happen.'

The old man shrugged. 'That is not my affair.'

There was obviously no point in further discussion and Kane changed the subject. 'Is there any reason why I shouldn't see the woman?'

Mahmoud shook his head. 'She is still under guard in her tent. I will take you to her myself.' As he led the way through the camp, he said, 'If you will take an old man's advice, be careful when you return to Dahrein. Skiros will not forget what you have done to him.'

He paused outside the tent that contained Marie Perret. The guard sat cross-legged in the shadows beside the entrance, head lolling forward over his chest. Mahmoud exclaimed in annoyance and prodded the man with his foot.

The guard rolled forward into the sand, face turning to one side. He was still alive, but there was blood on his neck behind his left ear, the mark of a heavy blow.

There was no sign of a struggle when Kane looked inside the tent, but she was no longer there, and he turned to Mahmoud and said, 'They have taken her with them.'

'But why?' Jordan demanded.

'A hostage until he manages to get safely out of the country, or a means of hitting at me.' Kane shrugged. 'The reason isn't important.'

Mahmoud touched him on the sleeve and the old sheik's eyes were troubled. 'I am shamed that this thing should happen in my tents. Naturally this absolves me from my promise to hold you here for a day.'

'No one is to blame,' Kane told him, 'but we must leave at once. Where is the Somali?'

'He sleeps with my bodyguard,' Mahmoud said. 'I will send him to you.' He walked back to his tent, and Kane and Jordan hurried towards the truck.

'What about the Cunninghams?' Jordan asked.

Kane shrugged. 'They'll have to fend for themselves for the time being. This thing is more important.'

He smoked a cigarette and considered the situation,

while Jordan checked that everything was in running order. It was about one hundred and twenty miles to Dahrein over dirt roads, and in places the going was rough. Skiros and Muller had a two-hour start. Unless they had a breakdown, it would be impossible to catch them before Dahrein.

Jamal appeared from the darkness, followed by Mahmoud and several of his men. The Somali climbed into the rear seat, and Jordan slid behind the wheel and pressed the starter.

As the engine roared into life, Mahmoud leaned forward and took Kane's hand. 'As Allah wills it, my friend.'

'Till our next meeting,' Kane said, and Jordan moved into gear and the truck shot away in a cloud of dust.

For the first hour, they followed an ancient caravan trail through the mountains, Jordan straining his eyes into the darkness, swinging the wheel violently from time to time as the headlights picked out boulders and other obstructions in their path.

Kane leaned back in his seat, one of Jordan's cigarettes smouldering between his teeth. Despite his long sleep, he was still tired, but from somewhere in the depths of him, he had summoned secret resources of energy, some mysterious vital force that was to hold him together long enough to finish this business.

At the end of the first hour, a strong wind started to blow in from the coast, cutting across the mountains, driving the curtain of cloud before it, and the full moon appeared, its rays drifting down into the valleys, lighting the way before them.

Jordan increased their speed now that he could see more clearly ahead, and they hurtled along the bed of a sterile, barren valley, zigzagging between large boulders, lurching from side to side.

An hour later, they moved out on to a man-made road, hewn out of the side of the mountain and roughly surfaced with small stones.

As Jordan moved into a higher gear, taking them forward in a burst of speed, there was a loud report from the rear, and the truck slewed dangerously close to the edge of the road.

Jordan switched off the engine with a curse. 'Blow-out! Might happen more than once on this blasted road.'

They changed the tyre and were on their way again within ten minutes, but this time Kane was behind the wheel. There was no room in his mind for thinking of what lay ahead. He focused everything on the road, in grim concentration. His mind became a blank and nothing existed except the truck and the road ahead, twisting and curving along the side of the mountain, gradually sliding down towards the coast.

There was no question that he couldn't keep it up –

no question at all. He sat hunched behind the wheel for mile after mile, hands slipping in their own sweat on the rim, until three hours later they came down into the great valley which opened into the sea.

He and Jordan had not spoken for hours, but now, as Dahrein came into sight, Kane said, 'What time have you got?'

Jordan glanced at his watch. 'About four a.m. You feel okay?'

Kane breathed several times to clear his head and nodded. 'I feel fine.'

'What's our next move?' Jordan said.

Kane frowned. 'I don't think they'll use the hotel. Muller's house is the obvious choice. It's more secluded.'

All was quiet as he took the truck along the road past the airstrip and moved in through the outlying houses down towards the waterfront.

Dahrein was shrouded in darkness and he turned the headlights full on as he drove carefully through narrow streets and twisting alleys, towards Muller's house.

At the end of the street, he halted and switched off the engine. 'We'd better go the rest of the way on foot.'

He reached for his sub-machine gun and led the way cautiously along the street. A lamp hung suspended over the door in the wall and beneath its light a travel-stained truck was parked.

Jordan touched the engine housing briefly. It was still warm. 'They haven't been here long.'

Kane nodded. 'I know, we made good time.'

The door was locked. For a moment he hesitated, and then Jamal touched him on the shoulder. When Kane turned, the Somali was leaning against the wall, legs braced firmly. Kane slung the machine gun over his shoulder and scrambled up on to Jamal's back. As he reached the Somali's shoulders, great hands seized his ankles and pushed.

He pulled himself over the wall and dropped down into the garden. There were lights on in the interior of the house. He stood in the darkness, looking up at the windows, and then he moved quickly to the door and unlocked it. A moment later, Jamal and Jordan were standing at his side.

He locked the door securely, pocketing the key, and they moved through the darkness towards the house.

EIGHTEEN

IT WAS QUIET in the garden and a slight breeze lifted coolly across Kane's cheek as he crouched behind a bush a few yards from the front door. He moved forward out of the shadows and mounted the steps to the terrace, followed by Jordan and the Somali.

The door opened to his touch and he walked inside, sub-machine gun ready. The light was on, and from upstairs, there came the sound of faint movement.

He turned to speak to Jordan and a door clicked open on one side of the hall. An Arab servant in white robes entered, carrying a suitcase. As he saw them, his eyes widened into saucers. Before he could cry out, Jamal took a quick pace forward and slammed his fist against the side of the man's jaw. He slumped to the ground without a cry, the case slipping from his grasp.

A voice called impatiently from upstairs and Muller appeared on the landing. 'For God's sake, hurry, boy!' he shouted, and then he saw Kane.

He pulled a Luger from his pocket and fired one wild shot that ricocheted from the wall, causing them all to duck instinctively, and then he turned back into his study and slammed the door.

Kane moved cautiously up to the landing and flattened himself against the wall. He reached over quickly and tried the door. It was locked. Jordan and Jamal crossed to the other side and they waited. Muller made no sound.

Kane nodded to Jamal and the Somali moved forward silently, fired a long burst that shattered the lock, and kicked the door open. He jumped back to the shelter of the wall, but Muller made no move. After a moment, Kane peered round the corner into the room. It was empty, and in the far wall, another door stood open.

It gave on to a back stairway and he led the way, moving cautiously down into the darkness. The door at the bottom was closed, and when he opened it, he found himself standing in the garden.

'Do you think he's still there?' Jordan whispered.

Kane nodded. 'He must be, I locked the gate, and he's too small to get over that wall without help.'

A bullet sang through the bushes and dunted against the wall a few feet away. They crouched down and Jamal moved in beside them.

'Don't be a fool, Muller,' Kane called. 'There are

three of us and we're well armed. You don't stand a chance.'

Somewhere, a bird, disturbed by the unaccustomed noise, lifted through the bushes, and there was an uneasy fluttering from the doves that perched on the roof of the house nightly.

'We'd better split up,' Kane told Jordan softly. 'This isn't getting us anywhere. But for God's sake, don't start any indiscriminate firing. You might get me instead of Muller.'

Jordan grinned. 'I'll be careful.'

Jamal moved away to the right and Kane started to crawl forward. The ground was wet with dew and he got to his feet and stood in the shadow of a fig tree, acutely aware of every sound. And then another shot was fired and Jordan cried, 'He's making for the gate, Kane! Head him off!'

Kane moved forward quickly and came out on to the path as Muller appeared some twenty or thirty feet away. The German ran to the gate and vainly tried to open it as Jordan emerged from the bushes and joined Kane.

The German turned to face them, despair in his eyes. He held the Luger close against his right thigh and Kane lifted the sub-machine gun. 'Don't be a fool.'

Muller raised the Luger and fired, and Jordan seemed to catch his breath sharply and stumbled sideways into

Kane. Muller raised the Luger again, and Jamal stepped out of the bushes and fired a burst that drove the German back against the gate.

Jordan's face was twisted with pain and Kane could feel blood trickling across his hand as he supported him. He called to Jamal and the Somali lifted Jordan in his arms and carried him back towards the house.

Kane was about to follow, when Muller groaned. He hesitated and then walked down to the gate and dropped to one knee beside the German. His eyes were open and glazed with pain, and his chest seemed completely shattered.

Kane leaned down and said urgently, 'Muller, can you hear me? Where are the others?'

But he was wasting his time. Muller's eyeballs retracted and blood erupted from his mouth. His head fell to one side and he lay still.

Kane stayed there for a moment, thinking, and then he dragged the body off the path into the bushes and unlocked the gate. He went back up the path to the house.

Jamal had stripped Jordan's shirt from his body. The bullet had caught him beneath the left breast, but a close examination showed that it had been deflected by a rib, scoring a deep groove in the flesh, which bled freely, but was not otherwise dangerous.

As Jamal tore the shirt into strips and quickly bandaged

the wound, Jordan opened his eyes. 'Don't worry about me,' he said. 'You've still got Skiros to think about.'

'After we've got you to a doctor,' Kane said.

As Jamal picked him up, the young geologist fainted, and Kane led the way down through the garden to the truck. The Somali eased Jordan into the back seat, then climbed in beside Kane.

As they drove away, the surrounding houses were quiet, and Kane reflected grimly that it was a fortunate thing that, in Dahrein, gunfire in the night was not so unique as to arouse comment.

He braked to a halt outside the hotel and Jamal followed him in, Jordan cradled in his arms. The foyer was deserted and a Hindu night-clerk dozed behind the desk. Kane grabbed him by the shoulder and brought him rudely awake.

'Where is Skiros?'

The Hindu spread his hands. 'He is away, Sahib. He has been away for several days now.'

The man was lying, Kane was sure of that, but for the moment, he let it go. 'Is Doctor Hamid still living here?'

When the clerk nodded, Kane went on, 'Give me a key for a room on the first floor and get him out of bed. Tell him it's urgent.'

The clerk moved round the desk, handed him a key, and went upstairs ahead of them. Kane quickly checked the number of the key, located the room and opened the door.

Jamal laid Jordan gently on the bed and stood back. Jordan's face was beaded with sweat, and as Kane anxiously examined him, the door opened and a thin-faced, greying Arab entered. He wore a dressing-gown and carried a black bag. He nodded briefly to Kane, pushed him out of the way, and leaned over Jordan.

He straightened up and opened his bag. 'Looks worse than it is,' he said in precise English. 'He's a lucky man, though.'

'I'll leave him with you, then,' Kane said. 'I'll be back later to see how he is.'

Doctor Hamid nodded impatiently, his mind already on the task before him, and Kane and Jamal left the room.

When they went downstairs, the clerk was back behind his desk, reading a newspaper. Kane went and leaned against the desk and waited.

The man looked over the newspaper and smiled uncertainly. 'There is something I can do for you, Sahib?'

'You can tell me where Skiros is,' Kane said.

The Hindu shrugged. 'As I have already told you, Sahib, I have not seen Mr Skiros for several days.'

'Normally I'm a patient man,' Kane said, 'but you've caught me on an off-night. Either you tell me where Skiros is, or I'll ask my friend here to break your arm.'

The clerk looked at Jamal and winced. 'That will not be necessary, Sahib. There is a limit to all things – even loyalty. Mr Skiros was here about an hour ago. He took many papers from his office and a quantity of money from the safe. He told me he was going away for a while, that if anyone asked for him I was to say I knew nothing.'

'Was Marie Perret with him?'

The clerk shook his head. 'He made two telephone calls, that is all.'

Kane glanced across at the switchboard and smiled. 'And naturally, you listened in to those calls.'

The Hindu shrugged. 'The first was to Professor Muller. Mr Skiros told him to hurry. He said that everything was arranged.'

'And the second?'

'That was to Captain González, the Customs Chief. Mr Skiros told him to come round at once and to bring all the money he could lay his hands on.'

'Did he come?'

'He arrived twenty minutes later. He was very angry, Sahib, but Mr Skiros threatened him.'

'About what?' Kane said.

The clerk shook his head. 'I am not sure, Sahib. It sounded as if they had been business partners.'

Kane stood there for a moment, a slight frown on his face, and then he nodded to Jamal, who had been standing impassively at his side, crossed the hall quickly, and went out into the street.

As they walked along the waterfront, many things became clear to him. The fact that Skiros had denied all knowledge of Cunningham's arrival in Dahrein was understandable, but that González had missed him was not so easily explained. The Customs Chief was lazy and shirked his duties, but every beggar in town was his spy, and little happened that he didn't get to hear about.

And what about all those times Kane had brought currency into Dahrein for Skiros? González hadn't searched the boat once, obviously because he'd been fixed by Skiros and they hadn't bothered to take Kane into their confidence.

They had arrived at the Customs Chief's house. Kane pulled hard on the bell chain and waited. After a while, there was a movement on the other side of the door and González peered out through the grill.

'Who is it?' he asked.

'I'd like a word with you,' Kane told him. 'It's rather urgent.'

Grumbling, González unchained the door. It opened slightly and Jamal kicked it back against the wall.

When Kane moved in through the gateway, González was sprawled on the ground. 'What is the meaning of this?' he demanded angrily.

Kane hauled him to his feet and pulled him close. 'Where's Skiros?'

Something very like fear appeared in the Spaniard's eyes, but he tried to bluster. 'How should I know?'

Kane held him with one hand and turned to Jamal. He spoke clearly and distinctly in Arabic. 'This dog knows where Miss Perret is being held prisoner. Make him talk.'

The Somali's great hands reached out and fastened around the Spaniard's shoulders. A second later, he was bent over one mighty knee, back arched. He screamed once and Kane moved forward and nodded to Jamal.

As the Somali relaxed the pressure, González stretched out a hand appealingly to Kane. 'Tell this black devil to leave me alone.'

'Not until you've told me what I want to know,' Kane said harshly.

'Skiros and the girl are on board Selim's dhow, the *Farah*,' González said. 'They sail with the dawn tide.'

Kane nodded to Jamal and the Somali dropped the Customs Chief to the ground where he lay, groaning with pain.

Kane hurried along the waterfront and turned on to the jetty. Several dhows were tied alongside, but there was no sign of the *Farah*. For a moment, he was filled with fear, and then Jamal touched him on the shoulder and pointed.

The *Farah* was anchored in the middle of the harbour. No other boats were moored in the vicinity, and moonlight carpeted the water with silver.

It would be impossible to approach in a boat without being seen, and they crouched low and worked their way towards the end of the jetty. Kane paused as he heard a slight sound.

He peered over the edge of the jetty and saw an Arab sitting in a dinghy, hidden in the shadows between two dhows. 'Is that you, Sahib?' the Arab called softly.

Kane realized that he had been mistaken for Muller. He started to climb down the iron ladder backwards and replied in a muffled tone, 'Yes, reach out your hand to steady me.'

He half-turned and kicked the man in the stomach as he stood up. The man subsided into the bottom of the boat with a groan, and Kane dropped down beside him.

He quickly peeled off his shirt. He was busy with the laces of his desert boots when Jamal joined him. The Somali squatted beside him in the darkness and Kane quickly explained the plan. When he had finished, there was a worried frown on Jamal's face, but he nodded reluctantly.

Kane stood up clad only in his khaki pants. He took the knife from the belt of the Arab sailor who lay in the bottom of the boat, pushed it into his waistband, and lowered himself into the water. He started to swim out into the harbour, using a powerful, but quiet, breast-stroke.

He felt naked and alone as he came from the shadows between the moored dhows and moved into the silver path of the moon. Luckily, a slight breeze was blowing in from the sea, lifting the surface of the water into tiny waves which helped to hide him.

As he approached the *Farah*, he could see the look-out standing in the bows, rifle slung from his shoulder. Kane swam quietly under the bowsprit and rested, hands firmly wrapped round the anchor rope.

After a moment, he started to climb, hand over hand. The look-out was standing on the other side of the deck looking towards the jetty. Kane climbed over the rail and moved on silent feet.

He hit the man hard across the back of the neck with the edge of his hand, and the Arab slid to the deck without a sound. Kane picked up his rifle and checked the action, then moved down the short flight of wooden steps that led to the waist of the ship. He paused in the shadows.

The crew lived in a portion of the hold and he peered inside the hatch. Voices were raised in laughter and there was a smell of cooking. He laid down the rifle and pulled the heavy storm cover of the hatch into place, securing it with metal brackets.

He started to get to his feet, hand reaching for the

rifle, and from behind him there came a slight creak. The cold muzzle of a revolver touched him gently in the back of the neck, and Skiros said, 'Very good, my friend. It almost came off.'

Kane turned slowly and the German smiled. 'So old Mahmoud didn't keep his promise to hold you?'

'Not when he found you'd taken Marie,' Kane said. 'You touched his Arab pride on the raw there.'

'A matter of indifference to me. I've been waiting for Muller. Presumably he won't be coming?'

'I'm afraid not,' Kane said.

Skiros smiled again. 'In a way you have done me a favour. He might have proved troublesome. You've only anticipated my own intention.'

'That I can believe,' Kane said drily.

Skiros pointed to the hatch. 'Now you can open it again. There seems to be no further reason to delay our departure.'

Kane removed the metal brackets as slowly as possible. He pulled back the hatch, and Skiros called, 'All hands on deck!'

The Arab seamen poured up from below and stood in a group, talking excitedly, eyeing Kane in an unfriendly manner. Skiros called forward one who was obviously the mate and ordered him to make sail, then he pushed Kane along the deck towards the stern.

He opened the door of the captain's cabin underneath

the poop-deck and pushed him inside. Kane remembered his last visit, the night the attempt had been made on his life by one of Selim's men. The cabin looked just the same. There were rugs and cushions scattered on the floor round a low brass coffee table, and underneath the great stern windows, a sleeping couch was freshly prepared.

Skiros stood on the other side of the table and sighed. 'If only you and I could have seen eye-to-eye with each other.'

'Hardly likely,' Kane said. 'You're finished. No great coup, the Suez canal still open. What will the Führer say?'

'He has other things on his mind. The Panzers rolled yesterday, my friend. Poland is already facing the worst defeat in Europe since the First World War.'

'I thought that was the one Germany lost,' Kane said.

Skiros scowled. 'Not this time.'

'I know. Tomorrow the world. What have you done with Marie?'

Skiros took out one of his oily black cheroots and lit it awkwardly with one hand. He chuckled, coughing heavily as the smoke caught the back of his throat. 'I find all this rather amusing. I never thought you were the type for love and romance and all that sort of thing.'

He took a key from his pocket, moved across to a

small door, unlocked it and stood to one side. Marie Perret moved out into the room.

For a moment, she stood there, dazed and bewildered, and then she saw Kane and came straight to him.

'Has he harmed you?' Kane said.

She shook her head. 'No, but I found his conversation as revolting as his person.'

Skiros laughed until the flesh danced across his great body. 'I wonder how you'll talk when your friend here is bait for the sharks out in the Gulf.' He thumbed back the hammer of the revolver and centred it on Kane's stomach deliberately.

Kane looked beyond the German, out through the open window, his eyes on the thick rope of the stern anchor. As he watched, something moved and two hands appeared over the edge of the window. A moment later, Jamal peered cautiously into the room.

Kane concentrated everything on keeping Skiros talking. He slipped a hand into his pocket and took out the knotted handkerchief that contained the necklace he had found in the passage leading to Sheba's tomb.

He tossed it down on the brass coffee table. 'Kill me,' he said calmly, 'and you'll be making the greatest mistake of your life.'

The German laughed harshly. 'Don't try that sort of stuff now. It won't save your skin.'

Kane picked up the handkerchief and started to untie

the knots. 'See for yourself, and this is only a sample. Sheba's treasure. We found it back there at the temple.'

He held up the necklace to the light and the emeralds glowed with green fire. The German's jaw went slack and an expression of awe appeared on his face. 'Holy Mother of God, I've never seen anything like it.'

He snatched the necklace from Kane's hand and examined it closely. After a moment, he looked up and a genial smile appeared on his face. 'In the right quarter, this will be worth a fortune. I'm obliged to you.'

They were the last words he spoke on earth. He started to laugh, his finger tightening on the trigger of the revolver, and Jamal stepped off the sleeping couch, arms extended.

One hand fastened over the German's mouth, the other struck the revolver from his grasp. Skiros started to struggle, but Jamal slipped an arm round his throat and bent him backward over one knee.

Panic appeared in the German's eyes and his legs threshed wildly. There was a sound as if a dry branch had snapped and he was still.

Marie gave a gasp of horror as Jamal lowered him to the floor and turned towards them. As Kane bent to pick up the fallen necklace, the stern anchor passed the window and the dhow moved forward as the wind caught the great lateen sails.

Kane gestured towards the windows and pushed Jamal forward. 'Quickly, there's no time to lose.'

The Somali slipped out feet first and disappeared. The dhow was already picking up speed as it moved towards the harbour entrance, and Kane pushed Marie through the window.

He looked back once at the body of the German, who lay with his face slightly turned towards him, eyes open, and then took a deep breath and jumped.

As he surfaced, the dhow was already moving away, and he started to swim towards Marie, who was clearly visible in the moonlight.

She waited for him, treading water. When he reached her, she fumbled for his hand and for a little while they stayed there like that, looking at each other.

The dhow moved out into the open sea, lateen sails billowing in the wind, and Kane looked again at Marie, and for some unaccountable reason, they started to laugh.

He held her hand very tightly and they turned and swam slowly together through the warm night towards the beach.

SIGNET

By the same author

EYE OF THE
STORM

The IRA, ETA, the PLO, Sean Dillon has worked for them all. His assassin's bullet is highly respected and highly priced. Now, in the middle of the Gulf War, the Iraqis need his services for a vicious terrorist strike: Target Britain.

The plan is to shake the world – wipe out key Western Government figures, and gain a massive propaganda coup. But on Dillon's tail are British Intelligence. They've found a killer to stalk a killer, a man with personal reasons to enter the storm … a man with bloody revenge etched into his soul.

'Compulsive reading' – *Daily Mail*

SIGNET

By the same author

THUNDER POINT

St John, the Virgin Islands, 1992 ...

For once, the lone diver's treasure was priceless: a German U-Boat, sunk in American waters three weeks after the end of the war. Inside: final proof that Reichsleiter Martin Bormann escaped from Hitler's bunker – with the Third Reich's hideous secrets intact.

Among them are the names of British Nazi sympathizers – some of them pillars of the establishment. For the sake of national security, the U-Boat must be destroyed. And no questions asked.

Even if that means persuading Britain's most wanted IRA terrorist to take on the job ...

Thunder Point is also available as a Penguin audiobook, read by Roger Moore.

SIGNET

By the same author

ON DANGEROUS GROUND

August 1944: a British Dakota on a flight from China to London crashes outside Delhi. Destroyed in the flames: a clandestine treaty signed by Lord Mountbatten and Communist leader Mao Tse-tung. An agreement to change the course of history ...

June 1993: in New York a doctor from a wealthy criminal family hears a startling death-bed confession. Could the Chungking Covenant have survived? And how much would the British and Chinese governments pay for its destruction?

'A splendid *Boys' Own*-style adventure – full of flying fists and whizzing bullets and beautiful but deadly women – in the tradition of Sapper or Alistair Maclean' – *Daily Express*